Funeral Party

till

Death

do us

Part

a

fictional story

by

Leigh Scott

edited by

Ashlynn Warner

Chapter 1. Initiation Fred 3-14

Chapter 2. Termination Kenny 15-28

Chapter 3. Biomagnetic Jamey 29-44

Chapter 4. Determination Rodney 45-65

Chapter 5. Disbarred Huston 66-84

Chapter 6. Marital Diss Gregory 85-89

Chapter 7. De-bassed Andy 90-139

Chapter 8. Death and Disguise 140-146

Introduction Disclaimer

This is fictional. If anything, or anyone resembles a real person or situation, it is coincidental. This was created from imagined interactions, characterizations and situations, not based upon any actual people or events. It is meant to be entertaining, for an amusing story.

Chapter 1. Initiation Fred

Leigh was always hellish. She was full of mischief early on, having almost a half dozen sisters - Julie, Angie, Jamie, Jeanie and Debbie - with dysfunctional parents. When their father was employed, he stayed out of state as a traveling salesman while their mother, who was a medical professional, stayed in an altered state. Their affiliation consisted of his infidelities and her addiction that neither could forgo due to the size of their brood, as a marriage of inconvenience. Without any parental guidance, there were so many pranks to commit. Too many females under one roof made Leigh a bit misogynistic from the mutual cruelty. She preferred the company of males as a tomboy. This set the agenda for her first attraction.

She was a scrawny, frizzy-haired, little, red-headed stinker. Being a teenager, who wanted a car, she devised a plan to come up with the cash to pay for her first car. Lawn mowing wasn't lucrative enough, and babysitting wasn't for her. She plotted her ideas, writing them down on a yellow pad. She researched how much money she needed and what kind of car she would buy, even down to the preferred color. This little yellow notepad became a point of embarrassment. Her older sisters found it and ridiculed her mercilessly, as she was only 14. They did not think her plans were possible.

That summer, she conspired with her oldest sister, Julie, to go to work with her in Downtown Atlanta. Being six years older, Julie was newly married and worked in a high-rise for a Stockbroker. She had arranged for Leigh to meet with two brothers who owned two competing sandwich shops in the lobby. Both brothers were in their mid-thirties. They were neatly trimmed and wore glasses and loafers. Their appearance served as a disguise to unsuspecting little girls. Leigh lied about her age and became employed, scooping ice cream and slathering cream cheese on bagels. The summer passed not quickly enough. She learned how to avoid each married brother in any confined space. One of the brothers came up to her from behind as she was bent over cleaning the ice cream freezers, forcibly pressing himself against her. Being her first job, she avoided conflict and any compromise by staying alert and quick so she could have them as a reference for whatever came next as her savings grew.

Being on track financially, Leigh opened a savings account at a local Savings and Loan. It was one of the first with an automatic teller machine - ATM. This made banking much easier, not having transportation yet. Tracking her own progress was now very private. Any documentation was kept secret from the sisters. The two older sisters, closest in age that ridiculed her the most, shared a room as well as an employer. Jamie and Jeanie worked at California Steak House. Since Leigh's summer job had ended with the start of school, she needed a new source of income as well as a regular ride to work. She applied at California Steak House as a cashier. They knew that Jeanie and Leigh could not both be 16, but they hired Leigh anyways. Jeanie was the fourth oldest. She had a dark complexion, as a tanned curvy brunette. The women had uniforms with a tight polyester orange and mustard color stripping vertically across the front to emphasize curves and a dark brown for a slimming appearance. The waitresses would utilize the zipper effect for enhanced tipping. Leigh had no curves in her zipper and did well to get a small enough size.

Being in high school, Leigh was only supposed to work parttime, but she picked up as many hours as she could as she tallied her bank account. Working with her siblings was an eye-opener. Jamie, the third oldest was a quick-witted, attractive petite young woman with thick auburn hair. She was waitressing as an art form, as in con-artist and seductress. She had been there for a few years and started dating an attractive waiter who had moved on to a more lucrative restaurant, Ed's Steak and Seafood. She followed him, and so did Leigh's ability to get a ride to work. Both Leigh and Jeanie were left without transportation and their mother was not always dependable. Jeanie was old enough to get her driver's license and resolve the dilemma. With parents as a co-signer, Jeanie financed her first car, a used 1976 Ford Mustang hatchback. It was tennis ball yellow and had no radio.

Now that Jamie was no longer the queen of California Steak House, Jeanie stepped up to the vacant throne and assumed the position. She ruled as the dominant flirt, working as a cashier and waitress, moving amongst the male employees, garnering as much attention and display of her sexual attractiveness. She ruled with crass jealousy over any other female who honed in on any male interests, like yowling, poofed-haired hissing cats, fangs, and claws flaring.

This was curious to observe in a sibling. Typically, you only knew them in a family setting, but this was without parental guidance and totally new to Leigh. She hung with the guys typically as a teammate, having a mutual interest in sports. This demonstrated something altogether strange and unusual, the conflict, difference, and attraction between the sexes and all of the ugly fallout as now Jeanie's reign was being undermined by her own sister, Leigh.

Being quiet and sneaky was Leigh's main suit. She was passive aggressive and escaped before a prank went past being fun. It was a difficult balance for Leigh to maintain, needing to have a ride to work and trying to keep Jeanie's jealousies and insecurities at a low heat. If any of the male suitors strayed, she was venomously vindictive. This created resentment amongst her co-workers and Jeanie became a mark to inflame. It became too amusing to the pranksters in her midst to not tease the wild queen of cattiness.

Part of a cashier's job description entailed food preparation. Having an extensive salad bar, it was an endless chore. Chopping a wide variety of salad accouterments', re-filling buckets at the salad trough, to preparing strawberry parfaits, making gallons of iced tea, spooning vats of whipped butter into little paper cups, and rolling silverware filled any time inbetween filling customers' orders and collecting funds. Closing was even more strenuous. Disassembling the salad bar, cleaning up any errant blobs of dressing and containing all perishables was something Jeanie took pride in. She could set up and break down the salad bar faster than anyone else wanted or cared to at California Steak House.

Carts of buckets from the salad bar were stored in a huge walk-in freezer along with pre-made desserts; large, drawerlike plastic, storage containers filled with various prepped vegetables in ice; and vast piles of cut beef. There was always a fear of being shut in the walk-in from Leigh's perspective, until she discovered others who used the seclusion for intimacy. It sort of took the edge off of some of the steamy interactions apparently. Another discovery was uncovered during inventory, the walk-in pantry was where the real action took place at room temperature.

Promiscuity was common with many of the older employees. It seemed to lighten their load of the old day in and day out adage. Again, this type of mixing of the sexes seemed consistent with Leigh's previous work environment. It was both shockingly curious and an interesting distraction for the co-worker's relationships on a mundane day to day, hourly earned life, enhanced by tips and lips. Now, Jeanie had several followers. Two brothers from Kansas thought she set the moon in the sky. Tom was the older of the two with coal black hair and eyes just as dark. He was attractive, with broad shoulders. His brother, Jeff, was even broader, with sunstreaked hair. One was a cook and the other was a dishwasher. They had been worshipping her for some time prior to Leigh's appearance.

They both viewed Leigh much differently than Jeanie. Leigh was one of the guys who were there to work and enjoyed an occasional food fight. Jeanie was distant and to be interacted with as she saw fit. Being the most beautiful, she did not have a hair out of place. Her makeup had to be just right. She was to be adored and fawned over while eating stolen cheesecake in the freezer, not to have food chunked at her like the rest of the monkey troop. She would scream so loud and so high pitched that it would draw a crowd in amazement at the wicked tirade that immediately followed any misstep. Now, this was too funny to witness without wanting to see more. Butter was the most egregious, being the most difficult to get out of your hair. Whipped cream was the most fun to fling on Texas toast, enabling greater accuracy of an intended target. Tom, Jeff, and Leigh created a war zone of flying food.

After work, the older employees would go to have pizza and beer together or to a local pub. On occasion, Jeanie would partake in these after hours, but Leigh was usually excluded, being so young. The longer Leigh was there, the more the work crowd began to shun Jeanie for her personality flaws and include the little sister in the antics and after-hours fun. Jeanie never had a handle on being cool. She took this very personally. Leigh could hang with anyone and not be judgmental. It was good. On one of these evenings, however, they decided to go to a local pub that had some live music. Being in a large group in a small town, Leigh was easily able to participate in libations with the locals. After a few drinks, the musicians took a break. Apparently, the singer was smitten with Leigh, demonstrating his immediate affection in a very public and very oral exhibition. She had to be scooted off the lap of the singer for the band. It was too funny to everyone when the older gentleman showed up at California Steak House the next evening looking for his lost little love. He was informed of Leigh's very young age and was never to appear at the steak house again.

Now, this apparently changed how she was viewed by her coworkers, kissing a complete stranger in public. This aroused another young man's attention, Ricky. He was a cook covered with acne. He was blonde but cute in an academic kind of way. He only worked weekends and attended Georgia Tech studying to be an engineer. He had his own place and thought he would start hanging with the homegirl. Leigh really liked Ricky and the attention from the co-workers, being included in the group. This enraged Jeanie. She was no longer the focus. How could her younger sibling be more interesting than her? She's not as pretty. She cannot compare to the curvaceous Jeanie. She couldn't even fill a uniform. But the variety of co-workers was as vast as it could, be and some of them were on the same team. This was unacceptable to Jeanie. It was bad enough that she had to compete with other women for men's attention but to compete with a man for men's attention was too far from her little world. The undercurrent was becoming obvious as Halloween was approaching.

Management decided that they were going to have a costume contest amongst the different California Steak Houses. This gave the employees a chance to express themselves like nothing else could. The waiters and waitresses prided themselves in the most sexually oriented attire, from French maids to odd Raggedy Ann's with cleavage. Not having a lot of shape to work with, Leigh came as a ghost with silver hair in a shredded sheet fastened as a gown. Most of the guys were vampires. Jeanie naturally was a black cat, in her bodysuit, furry ears, and dangling tail. One of the waiters became the center of attention as his alter personality; Michael became Michelle. She was so beautiful, she even had long blond tresses of a natural hair wig. She was a professional crossdresser and the belle of the California Steak House. She partook in augmentation, which really threw everyone off, especially the district Manager, who was the judge who thought he was in love at first sight. It was beyond belief to Jeanie that she was not garnering the attention, the spotlight as the sexiest, most gorgeous of the contest. She was unseemly furious to the amusement of everyone and the trick being played out on the district Manager.

It was such a memorable night at work that Ricky decided to have another party at his place, a toga party. He had been hanging out with the work bunch more to get closer to Leigh. She sensed his seriousness and began avoiding any one-onone scenarios, not joining in some of the after-hours, doing what she could to allow him to develop other interests with other co-workers. She was spooked and without a ride home. Ricky offered to take her home. He took her to his home. She was embarrassed by this situation, truly not wanting to offend him, but she was much too young for an adult endeavor. He understood and reluctantly took her to her home, being a complete gentleman. The next evening at work, he was already being targeted by one of the waitresses who moved in quickly for their consummation. After all, he was going to be more than just a cook. He was going to be an engineer. Leigh was quickly cast aside; her fame had waned.

At the toga party, everyone came in their own styled sheet ready to have fun. Ricky's new affiliation was talking about cohabitation and marriage. Wow, okay as heads spin. Alcohol and amusement had taken over as the pictures had later portrayed. Who was wearing what underneath their toga or not? Jeanie did not attend, but Leigh ended up finding a new suitor closer to her own age, Fred. All of the guys posed for a few pictures, one depicting all smiles in their sheets, the next mooning the camera. Ricky's tan lines were showing, trying to fit into the shot next to Fred who was taller with wellformed thighs that were spread a little too far, showing everyone all of his attributes.

Fred was a tall blue-eyed Italian with a mop of dark brown curls. He was muscularly attractive from his jawline to his toes. He exemplified masculinity, like a Greek statue, he was beautiful and used his desirability with a deadly gaze, fluttering his long lashes at his next victim. He drove an old Chevrolet from the 1930's. He was known for his pursuit of the virginal young ladies and now he had Leigh on his list of to do's. He had just broken up with a longtime girlfriend at school and needed a distraction for his broken heart. He would offer to take her home after work. He would hang out at her house. They would cook Italian food together. He was very attentive but could never seem to get her alone. He even would come by and take her to work. He would lie, claiming he ran out of gas, making the both of them late to work which got the both of them in trouble and caused the Manager to cut their hours. Leigh did not like this at all. This countered her whole purpose for working at the California Steak House to begin with. She pulled back, seeing that he was not interested in anything other than a virgin conversion, a game for him to win.

Jeanie was not happy at work with her sister. She was jealous of the attention Fred had given Leigh and now Fred was no longer taking Leigh to work. Jeanie had to be pressured into

it by their mother. This became more contentious as Leigh became more focused on her income. She would eat at home, not spending any money like everyone else at work. She had started getting more hours and Jeanie wanted less. On one payday, prior to their shift, checks in hand, Jeanie needed funds for gas money and agreed to take Leigh a couple of miles from work to her bank so that she could deposit her paycheck and provide Jeanie with some cash from the ATM after hours. Leigh got out and made the transaction, but Jeanie did not wait, abandoning her sister in the dark, miles from work. Leigh called her work, as Jeanie arrived on time without her sister. Another co-worker graciously came to Leigh's rescue. Jeanie's unwillingness to be transportation was immediately challenged by their mother and management. Change was coming for everyone.

Jeanie had started to have more of a nightlife, cruising with girlfriends. On one of these evenings, however, all did not go as planned. Neither Jeanie nor Leigh were working that night. Leigh was home, and Jeanie was out with a girlfriend. They had less than three beers between them, which was too much for Jeanie. At home, the girls were allowed to have a beer or two on occasion, so a little drinking was tolerated. At about 9:00 p.m., the telephone rang. It was Jeanie slurring her words in a panicky pitched voice asking if Mom was home. She had wrecked her Mustang! This was one of those memorable phone calls. Only their father was home, so Leigh ended up having to turn it over to him. He had a terrible temper and always made a bad situation worse, screaming, and yelling with the worst kind of cursing, condescending, blame, and belittling. The phrase "horse's ass in a wind storm" was usually included in the mix. It was always ugly dealing with him. The story was that the pair had 2 or 3 beers between them, compliments of her girlfriends' pilfering skills at home, and were cruising around. They ran off a jagged, curved road and hit a house totaling Jeanie's first car. It was later revealed that the house was about 20 yards from the road, and upon hearing the crash, the homeowner, who was a preacher, came out to see what had happened only to be verbally assaulted by the slurring Jeanie. Sure, the house was in the way, and that was the end of galivanting in the Mustang.

Shortly after the preacher's house episode, their father had found a new job. He had been out of work for quite some time. This is a real hardship for such a big family. However, this new job was in a new state, Texas. The new job meant selling their home, and moving their entire household, kids, and animals to an unknown place. Their folks found another house but did not have the closing funds they needed so, at the request of her father, Leigh turned her savings over to her father. He said it was a loan, that he would pay her back once they were settled in. It was over $5,500 that had taken her two years of part-time work to save.

After forgoing her savings and giving notice to California Steak House, having worked there for a year and a half, Leigh decided that she was going to make a change too. Not really knowing what to expect, she decided to have her first sexual encounter prior to the move so that she would know what everyone was making such a big deal about, why she had been pawed at, what it was about. She contacted Fred. He set up the rendezvous at Ricky's new love's apartment. Fred was very obliging and familiar with what would happen and explained the process to her in a very matter of fact way. This was conducted in such an uncaring, get it out of the way manor but she felt relief, not having this hanging over her anymore, having the knowledge and experience of what it was. Fred was only interested in his own enjoyment, finding pleasure for himself. He did not accommodate her in any way. She felt like sex was not enjoyable from a female's perspective. If that was all there was to it, what was all the hype about? He did nothing for her other than deflower her. Fred got what he wanted, and Leigh got away.

Chapter 2. Termination Kenny

The move to Texas severed off several of the sisters still at home. Julie had already found her new life. This created a need for Angie to return to Georgia to attend the University of Georgia within that first year, followed by Jamie shortly after.

A new high school in a new state in the 11th grade was too stressful with a dysfunctional home life. After all the work and effort put into saving for a first car, Leigh wanted to buy her first car but needed driver's education. Her father was wanting to control the process, having utilized her savings, he was willing to co-sign for her on a car loan. Starting over in the whole first car process with all of her planning cast aside, she had attempted to work as a waitress, but the hands-on training from her Manager exceeded her willingness to be groped. She ended up getting an after-school job at a local gift shop run by two married women with no issues of unwanted sexual advances. Leigh needed a car and worked toward what she had originally planned but would now have to make car payments. Both sisters, Jeanie and Leigh, now sixteen, ended up at the Department of Public Safety to take the written exam. Their father was so proud of his test score and was carrying on about how well he did and how smart he was, akin to Jeanie's self-absorption and their mutual narcissism. Neither could look in the rearview mirror without primping first. His test score was not the highest. This undermined his pride and dug into an old battle between Leigh and her father that had started decades before with their Mother. He regarded Leigh as a mini version of her Mother. Her father took out his anger on Leigh as the brunt of his rage. Instead of allowing Leigh to get a hardship license, he made her wait and take driver's education through school which wasn't offered until a year later.

Finding a suitable first car was not a mutually agreed upon situation for Leigh and her father. She had spent too much time planning for what she wanted to have him ruin her plans once again. They fought daily. He would find any discrepancy at home, and she would immediately be the culprit. Any cause to scream at her he would. After viewing dozens of vehicles, father was wearing thin, but Leigh finally found a repainted 1975 Datsun 280z that was agreed upon by both.

The longer the car sat in the garage, the worse the fighting became between Leigh and her father. You could feel the tension. His anger was intense. After passing driver's education, she was finally able to experience an unknown kind of escape from her father's tirades and constant disparagement. He originally stated he would pay her back the $5,500 she had saved but had only offered up the use of a gasoline credit card to assuage her inquiries.

Leigh was driving everywhere, exploring Dallas/Fort Worth, even driving to Georgia and back on weekends. Now in the driver's seat, the youngest sister, Debbie, needed Leigh to drive her to work. She tallied up almost $500.00 on the gasoline credit card, and her father blew up. He took back his credit card and retracted his promise to pay her the $5,000 she had loaned him to buy the house they all lived in, claiming that as far as he was concerned, she was into him for more than $10,000 as a 16-year-old minor. He did everything he could do to avoid his responsibility to the debt he owed her. She helped him out with the purchase their house. He pushed her out of his house and it became obvious that he would not be paying anything back aside from the gas card bill.

Debbie and Leigh started having little adventures together. They would cruise the local park hang out, the main strip where other teens loitered, stayed out late and drank alcohol. They would take a can of beer and had a plastic wrapper that would adhere to the can to make it look like a can of soda. If you looked closely, it actually said "coca-calo". In a pinch, Leigh would take a large fast food cup, put a can of beer inside, cover the sides with ice, open it, put a lid on with a straw through it to the can of beer there was nothing worse than ice melting in your beer. An open container was still legal and with Jamie's stolen driver's license, Leigh and Debbie were able to buy beer and get into clubs. This worked well until they ran into Jamie at one of these clubs. She ratted them out to the establishment, but this did not change things. They would get dressed up, put on a little makeup, and still could get what they wanted out of an evening. During this time, Debbie made a friend at school, Carrie. Carrie was into shoplifting and a guy named David. David was into Debbie, which created an interesting dynamic. David wanted to hang out with Debbie without Carrie, and he had a friend who was into drugs named Kenny.

Kenny was a 6'2", attractive, muscular, blonde without a clue. He was used to the ladies flocking around, which was obviously reflected in his self-assuredness and vanity. He was constantly primping and preening his long blonde locks in some reflection. He was from deep Oak Cliff, the South Dallas drug scene. Debbie included Leigh who had a car and was available to meet up with the boys. All four ended up in South Dallas, so Kenny could score some black mollies and crank. This was new to both Leigh and Debbie. David and Kenny had been well-versed partakers in the drug culture and had worked together at a local department store, Monterey Waters. The two young men had committed minor crimes and petty theft as a way to offset their dire poverty. Debbie had such a crush on David, but he was not into Debbie as much as she had hope. He seemed to be hiding something. He just wanted to stay away from home as much as possible. He was living in his mother's garage without any comforts, air conditioning or heating.

Kenny's home life was strange at best. He had a Thunderbird that his father had taken away from him. He had an older sister who had married a professional baseball pitcher, who had recently been killed in an automobile accident, and had plans for her pretty brother to marry up as well. His younger brother was a chubby religious nerd who suffered from asthma. His father was a retired Marine who supported his family on quarters he collected from sticker vending machines. His mother was a subservient, demure secretary for the railroad. His father was from a long line of Klu Klux Klan family members, who used to meet at a cement plant for their Klan rallies and subscribed to a Southern Baptist perspective. They lived in a 1,100 square foot house in the southernmost part of Oak Cliff. It was so riddled with crime, you couldn't park in front of the house without someone trying to break into your vehicle.

Leigh was not allowed to be in Kenny's house according to his very religious father. She had met Kenny's father who shook a bible in her face, blaming her for Kenny's transgressions, telling her she was going to hell, and she was condemning his son. He didn't realize that Kenny was teaching Leigh about the drug culture and sex. Kenny was very prolific and could easily be aroused with the least provocation. He was all about his own orgasms but did little else otherwise for Leigh. They had sex typically two and three times daily, like breakfast, lunch, and dinner. The two were constantly all over each other in public displays of affection and kissing. They typically would find a park but her car attracted the police, being caught with steamy windows after dark too many times. During the day, they would sneak into Kenny's house. His favorite place to have sex was in his parent's bed. Leigh asked him if that's where he was conceived. He would just grin widely, getting excited again. Leigh became more proficient at learning how to please her partner but never was given the same courtesy. Foreplay was non-existent, having to always be in a hurry before they were caught by someone somewhere. Again, the experience was a one-sided orgasm. He loved how she made him feel.

Leigh did not really care about drugs but was curious enough to want to know what was what. Debbie was more driven by her attraction to whichever young man suited her at whatever time. Kenny and Leigh became familiar with each other and spent any available time together, much to the dismay of Kenny's father. He would scream and holler about going to hell, quoting some bible verse, and that it was Leigh corrupting his beautiful son, his namesake as a junior. He seemed to be completely unaware of his son's drug dealing, criminal behavior, and illiteracy. The two had an ongoing war that Leigh had stepped into. His father took away his Thunderbird and had just sold it.

Dating Kenny was like having a human sex toy that would do anything at any speed without batteries. He wasn't a conversationalist. He was entertainment and as Leigh's home life worsened, alternative places to become the norm. She would avoid going home as much as she could and started skipping school, drinking more, and adding drugs to the venue. She raced cars and got speeding tickets to excess. She had paid off the car at this point, having paid for it twice but blew up the engine at high-speed racing. Being able to financially benefit off of her hardship and not being inconvenienced to repay his forgotten debt to her, the father agreed to co-sign on the new engine repair costs. This was only a delay to more bad behavior. She kept beer on ice in the car and was always going somewhere else she did not belong. She had become a regular with Kenny's criminal friends at a South Oak Cliff drug house.

Making beer and drug runs across the river was a well-worn path on the weekends. Across the Trinity River was the line for beer. There were liquor stores and beer joints up and down Harry Hines and the further you went, the seedier it became with prostitutes soliciting their talents and storefronts with painted windows that appeared run down and worn out like someone who was never going home again. Kenny and Leigh would frequent a drive-in style burger place that served Schlitz malt liquor in frosted mugs on a tray at your car. Another place to drink at that age was the Bronco Bowl bar. It was a hole in the wall of the South Dallas bowling alley that required a club membership. The two were such a cute couple that anywhere they went, they met little or no resistance to buying alcohol.

On occasion, one of Kenny's childhood buddies, Bob would come with them across the river for beer. Bob was a few years older, very scruffy from an even poorer upbringing with even more physical abuse than Kenny. They had grown up together with a bond of mutual suffering. Bob had an old Triumph motorcycle that he rode around everywhere in all kinds of weather. He let Leigh ride on the back a few times, racing down the interstate, wild hair everywhere, and the resulting tangles. He missed the one on one he had with Kenny before Leigh and had no one to care for him. His loneliness was so visible. Bob decided that he would quell this on one of those runs across the river. He had a few extra dollars from a new factory job out in Carrollton that was burning a hole in his pants. They picked up a pint of Chaves Regal and mixed it with Coke to garner courage. Leigh had only known of Chaves being consumed over ice by some visiting Priests invited to Sunday dinner. This time they cruised a little further down Harry Hines. Bob picked the store he wanted to stop at for some sexual release. He didn't get two steps in the glass front door before Kenny and Leigh watched as two partially clad women embracing him, stroking him with one hand while reaching in his back pocket retrieving his wallet with the other. He wasn't in there for more than 15 minutes but came out completely unfettered as he was still adjusting his pants and wallet, having been completely liberated of all of his funds and frustration from the working girls.

Working was not for Kenny. Kenny would get a job, but it wouldn't last long. He would rather steal and pawn than keep a regular job. He would suffer from asthma and miss work, not bothering to call in as a mean to become unemployed. Leigh started to attend night school for Real Estate and ended up dropping out of the 12th grade a few months before graduation. Kenny had dropped out a year before, so Leigh signed the both of them up to take a test at the junior college for their General Education Certificate, GED since neither had graduated from high school. Kenny was not wanting to take a test, but Leigh had already paid for them, it was all set up. He was relieved to find one of his former classmates taking the same test. He had copied his friend's test. Leigh was unaware how illiterate Kenny was until she bought him a birthday present with a funny card. He avoided the card and went right to the gift. After she asked him to read the card, he reluctantly opened it and stared straight at it with no eye movement and faked a smile, not having any idea what was written.

At a Halloween party, she went as Red Riding Hood with Kenny as the Big Bad Wolf. This ended once she became pregnant, and the party had to stop. Kenny was of no help for an adult situation and she had to decide what to do on her own. There had been too many drugs and too little alternatives to the commitment of having a baby. She sought an abortion at 17. Somehow, they were able to come up with a doctor in Uptown Dallas who would oblige without parental consent. It was blatantly obvious that things had to change. All of the weight and responsibilities were put solely upon Leigh. Kenny was incapable of any accountability; he couldn't even read street signs.

When Leigh was home at the same time as her father. They fought worse than ever. She was going to night school, working toward her Real Estate license and alternating with a night time job, and he would wake her as early as he could to assign blame for anything from parking in the driveway to leaving the butter out. Her mother cringed at the continuous battling between the two at home. As an effort to counter his harshness, Leigh was able to have Kenny spend the night on the couch, enabling her to not have to make the long drive back to Oak Cliff on the nights that her father wasn't home. When he was home, they fought worse than ever. All of this ended badly. Her father ended up taking away her car. He traded her beloved 280z, unbeknownst to her, for a 4 door Chevrolet Cavalier with a $5,000 note attached to it. There was seething hatred between the two, and he wanted to crush her, break her spirit completely. He could not make her take the car and ended up trying to pawn it off on another sibling.

This only emboldened Leigh, and now she seemed to have lost any and all restraint in their war. Nothing was out of bounds. Risk taking was another way to intentionally create more angst at home. During one Kenny's overnight stays, the pair ended up getting caught early one morning on a weight bench in the garage. Her mother felt she had been betrayed, and once her father found out, he had the opportunity he had been hoping for. He threw her out without anywhere to go.

At 17, she was too young to be able to rent an apartment on her own. She had no car and had to depend upon Kenny to borrow his father's car, which was not often allowed. She tried to stay at one of Debbie's boyfriends' apartment in Oak Lawn. The apartment complex was on the verge of condemnation. The tenants were drug dealers, pimps and the whores who worked for them. One of the working women she met had her apartment decorated in all in red with red paper parasols and Asian ornamentation. Everything, even she glowed in a red hue as she floated through each day with her Codeine addiction. She exclaimed that she had been a computer programmer at one point but could not do the day today. Doing this, she said she felt she had more control. Her book of business was catering to the Asian male populous. She had regulars but she had to watch out because they would try to cheat her upon payment for more than one at a time.

Her sister's boyfriend was a loading dock worker. He was a physically gorgeous idiot who was her entertainment. His roommate was also a co-worker, a huge American Indian. The two of them couldn't keep food in the house to satisfy their hunger. Fortunately, there was Sal's Italian across the street. Sal would make all of them calzones. Leigh did not eat meat, and he would make hers the size of a football. She would eat as much as she could, knowing any leftovers were devoured by the two hulking men. This set up did not last. She had no money and wasn't putting out to either. Her visiting boyfriend only emphasized that.

Kenny saw that Leigh was in a precarious situation and asked one of his friends, Bob if she could stay at his apartment in Carrollton. Bob was still appreciative of them accommodating him down on Harry Hines and agreed. He was working long hours and wasn't home much. Leigh would cook for him, and he and Kenny ate all they could. They enjoyed sitting back and relaxing together, getting high, and pigging out. Leigh was thankful to be out of the hole she was living in. She continued looking for work but being without a car made it a challenge.

The fourth of July was upon them. They got all of the fixings to make fajitas on a little hibachi grill on the patio. Leigh prepared the steaks for the grill and heated up cooking oil on the stove. A neighbor stopped by the patio for a visit and to smoke a joint. Everyone was partaking, and Leigh had forgotten about the cooking oil heating up. Everyone went from a state of comfort to a state of panic. The kitchen was ablaze, the unattended cooking oil had started a grease fire!

Kenny and Bob ran into the kitchen, and the flames were running up the vent over the stove as they both grabbed pots of water and dowsed the flames, choking it out. The kitchen was smoldered with steam and charred black completely. The sound of firetruck grew to a piercing presence with the rush of excitement as the firemen entered to see the blackened kitchen. They were amazed they were able to put out a grease fire with water and assumed they must have overwhelmed the source with water everywhere. Leigh was not able to stay at Bob's as a result. He was not happy and lost his deposit as a result.

Leigh had uncanny timing with an interview at an apartment complex, the Haystack in Grand Prairie. The Manager, John, ran an all adult apartment complex and needed a Leasing Agent who would work weekends. They had a keg at the pool every weekend, and she had just turned 18 a few months before. He was impressed with the fact that even though Leigh did not finish high school, she still had managed to get her GED and attend night school for Real Estate and property management. He even gave her a vacant apartment to spend the night in that evening. Kenny loitered, being her transportation during the interview, and was thrilled to stay with Leigh that night in their own apartment.

In the vacant apartment, neither knew what to do. The electricity was off so they tried opening the windows and sliding door but it was still too hot at 11:00 at night to be able to sleep on the floor. They ended up poolside, asleep on lounge chairs until dawn. Leigh put herself together and met up with John to work out a schedule. He informed her that she just had to turn the breaker box switch and turn on the thermostat for the air conditioning. This was the best news. He worked it out that she could lease an apartment at a discount. Additionally, the complex leased furniture, and he would furnish the apartment gratis as an employee. They put everything together. She had a furnished apartment and a job. She could manage without a car every day and get groceries with Kenny's visits.

Leigh had her own place. It was a small, ground floor, one bedroom with orange countertops in the kitchen. She had her own kitchen to cook in, her own bed to sleep in, but Kenny's visits became a problem. He would spend days at the apartment, mostly poolside, and dealing drugs or stealing anything he could pawn. He would have his friends over while Leigh was at work and eat all of Leigh's groceries and make a mess. She was so relieved once she had bought a tenants' used washer and dryer, her very own, first appliances, but this was quashed by his dirty laundry she had put upon her. He wouldn't contribute to any of the costs, and once the food was gone, he would go back home to Oak Cliff. She couldn't afford him. It was her struggle to just survive at that point. He had developed other distractions, having other young ladies to see during Leigh's working hours. It had become unbearable. He became jealous over the weekend events and the poolside keg. Tenants would comment that she always had a beer in her hand, she would hand it to who inquired, "Here, it's the same beer," warm and flat. She was supposed to keep an eye on everything over the weekends to make sure nothing got out of hand. Leigh knew everyone at the complex, from the druggies to the grandmas. This wore on Kenny. He accused her of what he was guilty of, infidelity. His behavior became too much when he barged into the Haystack Office and punched out a tenant on the porch for being too friendly toward Leigh. John was pissed and ran Kenny off. Leigh was completely humiliated.

She had to shed her boyfriend like dead weight. She had been trying to figure out how to get her own transportation and worked out a payment plan with a little tote the note car lot on a 1980 Datsun 200SX. It was a debt, but it was freedom from the blonde, bombshell dud. The salesman made the delivery to the office. Now, Leigh had managed to get a job, a place to live and transportation. She had her own little life.

She signed up for more night school, not having to deal with Kenny any longer. She needed more credits to get a Real Estate Agent license.

Coming back to her apartment one evening, Leigh caught one of the superintendents in the furniture storage shed where the unleased furniture was kept. He was selling furniture to the tenants and pocketing the money after hours. She reported him to John. After everything that had happened, and now this, it was not safe for her at the Haystack, and she needed to make a change. She continued leasing apartments but needed to find other employment. John had been as tolerant and helpful as he could have afforded to be. She ended up finding a job as a receptionist that had better pay and moved with the help of some of her Haystack friends into a third-floor apartment at a safer complex, the Fairways. It was closer to her new job in Irving. It was across the street from The Clubhouse with a view of the hot tub. It had vaulted ceilings and a corner fireplace, definitely a step up.

She had to furnish her new place a little at a time. Initially, she just had a coffee table and sofa table she had purchased at a local flea market, Trader's Village. She bought a used bed with a frame. She purchased an unfinished dining room set that Tom and Pelton helped her stain. She found a department store outlet that had great bargains on furniture, and the new apartment quickly became home. Her new job was amongst more discerning people, and she had to reevaluate her attire. She was never accepted as one of them and continued working toward her Real Estate license.

Chapter 3. Biomagnetism Jamey

Leigh went back to leasing apartments as an assistant Manager a little closer to home. The Shady Valley Apartments were old, and the tenants reflected a senior level of impoverishment. The very pregnant and cranky Manager always had a lit cigarette dangling from her mouth. She claimed that she had built-in filters for her unborn baby. Tenants streamed in and out of the office constantly complaining about plumbing and air conditioning problems. It was not something the Manager cared or worried about, and Rodger, the superintendent, would set his work agenda based upon who had the best weed while Leigh tallied the rent rolls, gave late notices, and handed the to be evicted over to the Manager. There was always someone being put out on the curb.

While Leigh was at the Haystack, she had made some friends who kept in touch. They would get together and have taco eating contest after getting too high. They always smoked, especially Tom and Pelton. They stayed that way. The two shared an apartment together. At one point, they caught their furnace on fire, forgetting that they had hidden their stash in there. Another one of the regular boys was a tall lummox of a blonde, Jeff, who lived with his parents at the Haystack. He was almost 30 and was finally getting his own apartment. So, the guys wanted to get a couple cases of beer and help Jeff move into his new place. Sure, sounds like a plan. After all, they had helped her move too.

Jeff was moving into Fox Chase Apartments, a new place with someone new, a lanky, long-legged, long, frizzy-haired guy with big, green eyes named Jamey. Everyone in the room chokingly paused as they felt his presence. He directed his attention with laser precision on Leigh. He truly gave off an energy, a biomagnetism unlike anything she had never known and everyone felt it.

Moving forward to get the pending task done, they all pitched in to get Jeff situated, and once all was settled, Jamey opened the bedroom door and let out a big black and white cat named Bud. He explained that Bud was blind. The cat very gingerly made his way slowly around as Jamey stayed by his side, talking to him, comforting him. Jamey had an odd mix of floral furniture and a large slice of a lacquered tree trunk for a coffee table. He had homemade ceramics decorating the mantle, Cat Fancy magazines, plants, and ugly avocado green and yellow crocheted doilies and towel accents, not the typical bachelor's decor. Jeff did well to have a bed and some clothes. Moving Jeff was done and everyone was polishing off the last of the beer in no time. They watched in amazement as Jamey would throw crumpled up cigarette packages across the floor for the cat to retrieve. He picked up Bud and carried him outside in the grass, placing him down while talking to him so the cat could slowly walk around outside staying next to him. Jamey invited everyone back for a party at a later date. He said his friends would be coming down from Oklahoma for it; it would be fun. Sure, another reason to drink and smoke.

Jamey was sure to ask Leigh if she would come back by. He wanted to see her again. She agreed and they began their visits, which usually consisted of hanging out at his apartment after they both got off work. He loved to cook fried chicken and show off his domestic skills. He was a complete gentleman and never pushed Leigh for more than conversation and a little intimacy. He would be all showered and dressed up for her visits. It was very sweet, very thoughtful. Though he likes to smoke cigarettes and weed, he did seem very responsible compared to what she had known and was a little older at 27 to her, now, 19. He said he was divorced. His father had been in the military, and they had traveled all over the world. Jamey was born in Bogota, Columbia. He had lived in France and Germany too. He would tell her stories about spiders as big as dinner plates in Columbia, about the life he and his family led, about the beauty of Germany, the cultural differences, and how shockingly different Oklahoma was to him. He had a different background and style than anyone Leigh had known. He wore women's clothes and jeans, but she just chalked it up to a more European approach.

Jeff would often irritate Jamey during these visits. Both were always looking for a lighter, constantly smoking something. Leigh did not really care for smoking of any kind. They would be in the middle of an argument on several occasions when she would arrive, yelling and accusing each other of taking something or eating something of the other's. Jeff was angry with Jamey, Leigh was supposed to be Jeff's friend according to Jeff, he knew her first. Uncomfortable, she started stealing their lighters, completely undetected, making it more difficult for either to smoke those nasty little nicotine sticks.

On one of these visit's, Jeff wanted to borrow Jamey' car. Jeff had a little truck and didn't like the split seats for a date. Jamey reluctantly agreed. This was the beginning of Jeff and Patty. Jamey referred to her as Cow Patty. She was a little blonde who seemed to really be into Jeff, but Jeff was just into sex. She became pregnant. Jamey and Jeff fought about that too.

Leigh and Jamey had been seeing each other for a couple of months without actually having sex. He was a little put off by her being only 19, younger than his baby sister, but that didn't stop him. He was getting excited about having his friends meet his new friend, Leigh, at his party in December.

Leigh was enjoying the slow pace and included her younger sister Debbie in some of the visits to Jamey'. He seemed to be on his best behavior. It was too odd, but it was a nice distraction after her last break-up. She had been with Kenny for 3 years. Jamey seemed to genuinely care about Leigh. He would usually talk about his work as a welder and how capable and talented he was in his trade. He spoke about how he used to make a lot of money working for oil companies in Oklahoma but how the market fell out. He mentioned that his father, Jamey Sr., worked in Fort Worth, and that his mother lived in Oklahoma City. He had been in the Air Force for a short time and had gotten an honorable discharge but was unclear about why. He had two older sisters, a younger brother, and even younger sister, Debra. She was coming to the party too.

Leigh would often tease Jamey about his roommate, stating that they were so cute together. She had quite a stash of stolen lighters as the infighting intensified between the two. She would tell Jamey dead cat jokes, noting his excessive sensitivity to his cat. His cat was part of his divorce. His former wife, Lori, was into Maine Coon cats. He would talk about her and how heartbroken he was. She had been going to college and kept notes, a diary. When he lost his job in the oil field business, she wanted a divorce, because he could no longer provide well for her. However, he found her diary, and upon reading it, discovered that Lori was having an affair with another man. She a was tall, buxom brunette he obviously was still in love with. Leigh figured this was part of his dilemma, moving so slow in their relationship.

The evening of the party, it had turned cold as his Oklahoma friends started streaming in the door. They were very hardlooking biker types, scraggily-bearded and covered with tattoos, reeking of pot. One of his close friends, Rex, was very friendly, really cared about Jamey, and had an unresolved longing for Jamey' baby sister, Debra, who looked like the female version of her brother. She was very much of the drug culture Leigh was surrounded by. There was a haze settling over the apartment from all kinds of smoke, joints, bongs, and bottles of hard liquor. Now Rex wanted to have shots of crown with Leigh. Leigh did not drink much hard liquor, but she did not turn away from the challenge. She was out after about 4 in a row, but the party continued without her as she was tucked away into Jamey' bedroom, on his waterbed. There was a punch that fumed from the various mix of alcohols they consumed. The weather worsened as the party raged on. It began snowing, which did not dissuade the streakers as they made their laps around the complex to the hot tub and back.

Leigh woke the next morning undressed in bed with Jamey. It was obvious that he had taken advantage of her situation. She was really surprised after so many months, she thought she could have trusted him but now was completely dismayed. He had nonconsensual sex with her, as she laid passed out in his bed. She tried to make as little of it as possible and get back home. There were bodies passed out everywhere. Beer bottles were strewn about, cigarette butts overflowing from ashtrays with a stench of stale smoke and booze. She had to watch her step through the landmine of party ever after.

After the party, Jamey did not hold back from seeking more intimacy. Leigh did not know that his divorce had just become final, hence the impetus for the party. That had been the reason for his self-restraint. She was totally unaware, and he had intentionally kept it from her. It was all about the money. Oklahoma is an alimony state, unlike Texas, something she was learning about in her night class for Real Estate.

Being older, well-traveled, and now divorced, Leigh expected Jamey had a better understanding of sex. No one was in a hurry, and no one was trying to hide from someone. The more relaxed approach greatly enhanced Leigh's sexual awareness. Jamey liked to get high and have sex. This took away Leigh's nervousness and anxiety. She was finally able to climax and Jamey made fun of her for it, claiming that she was like a dog in heat. This hindered her ability to achieve any mutual sexual candor in their relationship. He became critical of her, claiming that her legs were like sequoia forests if she did not shave immediately preceding any intimacy between them. He would talk about his ex-wife having the most beautiful big, breasts and how smart and clever she was, intentionally making Leigh feel inferior.

Now that Jamey was single, he wanted to see Leigh's apartment. She was getting ready when he arrived for their date to actually go out to dinner. She let him in, offered him a beer and scurried off to finish getting ready. He was talking to her from the from the other room and started looking around her apartment. He notices a metal box on the fireplace mantle. He opens it. He hollers "Oh my God, my lighters!" Leigh peeks around the doorway laughing at his discovery, "Oops!" He was shocked. After all that time and fighting with Jeff, here they all were.

Jamey wanted to find a Chinese restaurant. She knew of one that served mixed drinks. The entrance had a circular carved motif with dragons in red and gold accented with aqua trim. It was a little dark but curious place with very traditional decor and hand painted lanterns for effect. The chalkboard at the door was advertising a free dragon glass with an order of two Mai Tais. That was for them. He was not happy that they did not have Peking Duck, but the two enjoyed their drinks and meal together. Their Mai Tais were served in an aqua ceramic mug with an undulating dragon wrapped around it. It was really impressive. Upon receiving the bill, they were given a bag with a clear tall glass that had a red dragon laminated on it, not at all like what they had been drinking out of. They got up to leave, putting a tip on the table, but

Leigh excused herself to the ladies' room while Jamey went to pay. She mentioned she'd meet him at the car. As he started up the car, Leigh appeared from the restaurant, climbing into the car. Jamey kept mentioning what a gyp the dragon glass was. Leigh started to laugh, pulling out the infamous ceramic dragon mug they had admired from underneath her shirt. He was shocked and thrilled. She had pilfered it for him.

They started spending all of their spare time together. The more they were together, the worse his relationship with Jeff became. They were wanting to split, and now Jeff was going to be a father with Pattie's baby. On top of that, Jamey' cat had become sick.

Bud had to be taken to the veterinarian. He had a severe urinary tract infection. Jamey had been warned by the vet to not give him cat treats, that it clogs up the poor little cat, but Jamey did not heed his advice. It was divulged that the cat had become blind because it had gotten into someone's marijuana, causing it to lose its eyesight. Leigh felt terrible. She had been teasing him with dead cat jokes for months. Bud ended up dying. Jamey was devastated and had a huge vet bill he could not pay. The vet offered to let him pay it out. Jamey knew Leigh felt bad, and she had a credit card. He asked if she would pay the vet bill, and he would pay her back. He now wanted to have his beloved cat buried in a pet cemetery, again requested that Leigh put in on her charge card, and he would reimburse her. It was several thousands of dollars for a cat. She never heard a peep out of him again about repaying her. She ended up making a friend of the veterinarian though.

Jamey had taken advantage of Leigh's compassion and the relationship started to turn into a very different situation. Neither had taken any needed precautions concerning birth control, and now Leigh was pregnant. Jamey was livid. It was all her fault in his mind. Now Leigh could not justify what she had done previously under similar circumstances. Furthermore, the guilt and anxiety from before was still too overwhelming to repeat. She decided, with or without him, she would proceed with the pregnancy. He became very spiteful, hateful, and mean. He felt like she trapped him intentionally. The extended family handled it varyingly, ranging the full gamut from great to awful. One of Jamey's sisters whom Leigh had never met claimed she was pregnant by their father instead. Leigh had not yet met the rest of his crew, but that changed too.

Jamey's father, Jamey Sr., worked in an industrial truck repair shop in Fort Worth. He lived in an apartment above a garage and would walk across Lancaster Boulevard to a little neighborhood pool and dance hall. Everyone called him Dusty, because he liked to dance with the ladies. He was a regular there. Jamey and his father ruled the pool tables. The two of them together rolled through a game so fast, if you looked away, you missed it. They laughed at Leigh's lack of skill in billiards. Jamey' parents were still married but lived separate lives. His father would send his paycheck to his mother and she would dole out his portion. Their marriage was marred by many decades of mutually toxic behavior. At one point, Jamey's father took Jamey and left the rest of the family behind, abandoning them and kidnapping Jamey.

Because he was in the military, this situation was resolved, and he had to return to his wife with their son.

Jamey's mother lived in Oklahoma in their family home, a typical brick, ranch style home. His youngest sister, Debra, moved in and out, depending upon her love life. His oldest sister, Kimberly, lived nearby and had two children. His second oldest sister, Donna, lived out of state and was unhappily married to a Manager of a famous rock band. His younger brother, Marty, was living in California. He was totally different than the rest of the bunch. He was actually Jamey's half-brother by an affair his mother had when they lived in Columbia.

Jamey's mother, Jane, was very gracious to Leigh. She was genuinely the most courteous of the family to her. She was from Germany. She towered over everyone, having a large build. She loved to stay up late and watch Johnny Carson. While Jamey and Leigh visited, she would give them her bed to sleep in. She was always trying to feed everyone. She was excited about having a grandbaby.

Leigh's family was cordial to meeting Jamey the first time. They emphasized the importance of having the baby baptized in the Catholic Church. Jamey was on his best behavior. It was tense and Leigh was distant to her parents. Her sisters were busy with gossip. Her Grandmother, Jane was the only one of the family truly excited about the great grandbaby but stressed that the two should get married. She began making plans for providing for the coming baby, buying a crib and crocheting a baby blanket.

The more Jamey and Leigh were together, the worse Jamey would treat her. He would openly pursue other women in front of her, unabashedly. He had no respect for her or her situation being forced upon him. He never moved in with her and kept his life separate. That first Christmas they spent together underscored how much he abhorred her. He refused to participate in getting a Christmas tree. She got one by herself, very pregnant and dragged it up three flights of stairs while he was sprawled on her couch in front of the television. A neighbor saw her and helped open the door to see Jamey just lying there. Jamey immediately feigned being asleep, embarrassed by the neighbor's glare. The baby was due Christmas day and was born the day after. She was named Jane, after his mother and her grandmother. Jamey started threatening Leigh, that he would take their baby and leave her. She became very fearful, dissolved her lease and moved back in with her parents. Her parents helped her find an attorney and set up child support payments with Jamey through the court system.

While she was back under her father's roof, she became a licensed Real Estate Agent and started working for a local Brokerage on straight commission. Old problems resurfaced with her mother's addiction and her father's abuse. Childcare became a serious problem. She couldn't depend upon anyone else, and her income was negligible. She ended up moving out. She found an old run-down house that she could live in, agreeing to fix it up and repair it as a form of rent. It was very dilapidated and didn't have air conditioning, and only had space heaters. She and Jane made it through the winter, huddled in front of one of the space heaters.

She had gotten an hourly job to have some income to be able to pay for child care, while still attempting to sell Real Estate. She could barely pay the electric bill and buy food. At the end of winter, the hot water heater went out. She didn't have any money to spare and ended up calling Jamey for help. She had not seen him in over 2 years. He never bothered with spending any time with their daughter. He repaired the plumbing, but the two had spent the one night together and Leigh became pregnant again. He was in total disbelief. He had been busy with other pursuits and thought she had been doing the same but that was not the case.

Leigh could not stay in the ramshackle old house with a new baby on the way. She found a little duplex and a better paying job as a telemarketer, enabling her to get through her pregnancy and afford childcare. She had to give up on her Real Estate career, being unmarried and pregnant was not permissible. She had just gotten an award for listing the most Real Estate in the Dallas/Fort Worth markets for her Brokerage and had to give up her listings to another Agent. She won a trip to Corpus Christie for her efforts.

Leigh's new place was much more suitable for the little family. They were very settled for the arrival of baby Marie. Jane was a very loving big sister. With another Christmas coming, came another surprise. Jamey showed up, wanting to be a part of their little family. He spent time with Jane and took her out shopping. They came back with a Christmas tree. He seemed very different than he had been before. He had come back into their lives with no real explanation, and he would disappear for days at a time. When he would show back up, he would be exhausted and sleep for days. He had purchased a new sports car, but it was unclear where he was working. A day after he purchased it, it was stolen. He had not had a chance to get any insurance on it so Leigh called her insurance company, and they covered the loss. She ended up locating the vehicle afterward. She also discovered that Jamey had been driving to Oklahoma and had started trafficking cocaine through his baby sister. This was not something she would allow in her little family and threw him out. Leigh had to sue Jamey for additional child support but he resisted and required a paternity test. The results verified her fidelity in the face of his discontent. He was beyond furious, not wanting to be accountable for his actions.

Leigh moved back into her parent's home trying to pull her life back together now with 2 children to support. All of her sisters had moved out, and now the two parents were seeking a divorce after 29 years of marriage. Her father had moved his mother in, so it was the 2 of them against Leigh and her mother. It was an ordeal. Leigh helped her mother find a condominium and filled any void that would have typically been done by her father.

Leigh had sought a new job. She decided to try to work for a builder. This would enable her to have some type of draw and insurance instead of just straight commission and still be in Real Estate. This worked well with the exception of having to work weekends and finding childcare. She was earning enough income and decided that she would try to buy a house. She found a little 2-bedroom, brick home in a quiet, little neighborhood for her little girls. They had a place to ride their bikes and a fenced yard to play in. It was so nice to have their own home. They planted flowers and had a garden.

Every two years or so, Leigh would have to go back to court regarding non-payment of child support. Jamey was not reliable and never had anything to do with his children willingly. The stress of dealing with him was very difficult. After one of these state-mandated proceedings, Jamey showed up again at Leigh's door wanting to try to be together again. He claimed he had stopped the drugs and would do better. Leigh was not really able to trust him again, but for the sake of the girls, she did try to let him come back into their lives once again. He still had his sports car and now wanted to park it in her little garage, still worried about it disappearing again, especially with the type of company he had kept.

Being Texas, they had just had a hail storm, and everyone had to replace their roofs. Leigh was expecting a roofer to give her a bid on a new roof. When the doorbell rang, Jane beat her mother to the door. The man at the door recognized her, but Jane didn't recognize him and ran across the street to get her girlfriend. They both came back to stared at this new stranger. Marie hid from him. They had not known any father figures and found it to be rather strange. It was Jamey. He had pleaded to come back. She opened her home to him once again.

One evening, Marie was not quite 2 and was climbing in and out of a laundry basket. She ended up falling, splitting the bridge of her nose open on a potted planter. Leigh and Jamey scooped up the kids and sped off to the hospital. Marie had to have stitches. It was fortunate that their father was there to help.

Leigh wanted to believe he could be better, that he could actually love them, that they could be a complete family. Jamey wanted to have a night out with Leigh. They had not gone out together since before she had children. It had been over 5 years. She couldn't help but be skeptical. They got a sitter and went to a concert. During the show, Jamey had disappeared and when he finally showed up, he was high. She was pissed and left him then and there. She got home and pushed his car out of her garage into the street and threw his clothes into the front yard. She had no tolerance for drugs in her family. She had too much of that growing up with an addict. He ended up showing up later that night and collected his things and left. He wasn't heard from again until another few years had passed and he was summoned back to court over non-payment of child support again.

Leigh did what she could to try to balance her family life with her adult life. She would keep them separate, but it was not easy, being alone, raising two children. She would have a night out and go listen to live music, go dancing or just try to have some fun with other adults. She really didn't have anyone else in her life other than her mother, and the two of them were often at odds over her mother's addiction issues. It was as enjoyable as it was as difficult. The girls were such a joy. Leigh, her mother, and the girls would spend Saturday evenings together. They made each other's lives better than they would have been alone. Leigh's mother stayed sober being around the girls so much, and the girls really enjoyed the love she gave them in return. It lightened the weight on Leigh as well, having some help with all of her responsibilities.

One of the most difficult situations occurred with one of the girls. She had been harmed at a babysitters' and Leigh had to make a change. Working weekends had to stop. She had heard about another single mom that was able to get student loans and get a degree. She had been able to qualify for financial assistance, and Leigh decided to give it a try. She was excepted into the local University and was able to get financial aid and worked as a work-study. She also was able to get child care assistance through a charity. She went fulltime and the girls became very familiar with the University of Texas at Arlington, being regular visitors as mom's assistants in her work-study jobs. Leigh was always hurrying off to pick up the girls from school, run to class, pick up the girls to go home, and back again. It was hectic.

Chapter 4. Determination Rodney

Needing a little adult time, Leigh decided she needed to have a night out and went to listen to some live music in Deep Elum. There were two different venues playing simultaneously. She would listen to one for a few songs then she walked around the corner to the other and check out what they were playing, trying to decide which was better. Going back and forth, she attracted someone's attention at a restaurant in-between, Parrot Joe's.

An attractive guy stopped her at the corner and asked if she would come inside the restaurant. The owner wanted to buy her a drink. She responded with "Okay, sure".

Rodney was a little taller than Leigh and full of fire, constantly smoking with a dark wavy head of hair. He was very confident, and his friend went out of his way to point out a wall mural in the restaurant that had Rodney's name painted on it as a proprietor. It seemed odd, like she needed proof of what she was being told. Rodney was not what he represented himself to be, but he did garner her interest and seemed to be somewhat entertaining and 9 years older.

At first, he was a good distraction from all school work and parenting. He was very playful, child-like, but very intelligent. He had a Master's in electrical engineering, but no discipline. He had tried to run another nightclub, lighting, and sound business, but all had failed. He loved Leigh's car. He would always have her meet him at the restaurant, and she never saw his vehicle. The first time she saw where he lived, she was shocked at how messy he and his roommate were. She had never seen someone live in such a disaster. The floor was covered. They were seriously lazy.

Rodney had a confidence that extended from his testosterone. He was the unexpected. He did not confide in Leigh about his awareness and experiences. He was secretive. She didn't really feel like she could trust him. He was acutely aware that he did not affect Leigh despite his endowments. He became uncomfortable about not being able to get her to climax. She would do all she could to try to put him at ease, pleasuring him with great care and emotion, but trust was the inhibitor for her. She could reach into his eroticism and achieve his satisfaction but, he could not understand hers. He wanted more control but couldn't figure out how to dominate her the way she dominated him. He would try to create situations that were edgy, having sex in risky places, hoping to entice her into a greater sensual experience, but having sex in a public bathroom wasn't anything more than a red-faced dare.

He didn't really talk about things or have any conversations of substance. Both seemed to always be distracted with either school or the restaurant. They never had any depth to the relationship. He had a difficult relationship with his father as well and had flunked out of military school. He claimed to be the founder of the gang "Freaks of Texas". His divorced and newly remarried mother favored his older brother over him and his older brother was, as he described him, a "lady killer", and he was. Jay was one of the most attractive men Leigh had ever met. He was jaw-dropping. He was tall, swarthy and handsome, had dark wavy hair and gorgeous green eyes, tanned with a beautiful smile. He was all testosterone. Rodney was always in his brother's shadow.

Leigh had lost Rodney's phone number, and there was no record of it with information. Rodney had created a fake identity under the name Grover Cleveland for telephone service. Rodney was always working against the system, never doing things the right way. He had a deeply rooted dyslexia of his physical and emotional sense. He had lost his driver's license as a result of this approach and ended up being arrested and incarcerated for a month by a harddealing Judge with no mercy.

Once Rodney was set free for time served, Leigh wasn't really comfortable with him behind the wheel. If Leigh could not come out to play because she didn't have child care, Rodney would invite her to bring her children along. That was new. She had always kept her adult life separate, but now her life was so hectic with school and the kids, it made sense to condense things a little. He was a lot of fun with the kids. He actually played with them, included them, and was really still one himself. Whenever just Leigh and Rodney had an actual date, Rodney seemed to come unglued fairly easily. He had a horrible temper. He would scream at people with the least provocation, much like her father. It scared her. Something wasn't right. Leigh never could put her finger on it. He would refer to Leigh's children as little monsters. She was hurt by this.

On nights Rodney had to work, but Leigh could get her mother to keep the kids, she would hang around the restaurant and the other local bars, listening to live music and enjoying a break for the pressures of school and parenting. On one of these late nights at a place across the street from the restaurant, a strange man was trying to talk up Leigh. She wasn't interested and Rodney was still at work at the restaurant. The man slipped something to the bartender. The two knew each other. Leigh ordered a bottled beer and saw the bartender turn away from her as he opened the bottle. It looked suspicious, and it was. She had become sick after one sip and ran back across the street. She found Rodney in his office. She became incoherent and vomited into a trash can. She had been drugged, but was, fortunately, able to get to somewhere safe. Being a woman alone in a club had become very risky.

One night Rodney took her out. They got all dressed up to go to a well-known seafood restaurant on lower Greenville. No preplanning was done. The restaurant was filled to capacity and the hostess offered to add them to a list with over an hour wait if they would be interested in going to a bar two doors down and having drinks while they waited, and that she would come and get them once a table was available. They agreed. Sure enough, a Martini later, she retrieved the couple as promised and brought them back to the restaurant, but someone else had already been seated at that table. Standing in the middle of the floor, the woman apologizes, but Rodney loses it, loudly barraging this poor woman, waving his arms, being very threatening, cursing, and especially embarrassing. Leigh was red-faced and ran outside to get away. He stood in the middle of the floor after his tirade, waiting for Leigh, who he thought had gone into the ladies' room, with all eyes staring at him. Leigh stood outside for what seemed like an hour before she poked her head back in and signaled to him. He came out and started in at her in front of the restaurant with everyone watching this lunatic. She was even more humiliated and in tears. She just wanted to go home and pleaded with him to just take her home. He refused and took her to another expensive restaurant with her smeared mascara in her distressed state. After dinner, he still would not take her home. It was too early. So, he took her to another club, and he got totally polluted, obviously not caring about her as a stranger walked up to her and groped her without any reaction from him. It was a bad date that had gotten worse.

As a way to avoid being alone with Rodney and his bad behavior, Leigh invited Jeanie to come with them to Deep Elum. Rodney knew all of the other proprietors, having worked there for so many years. They began their clubhopping, getting primed at Parrot Joe's. Jeanie would sit at the busiest corner of the bar. She would sit up, chest out, dress seductively positioned for optimum effect, legs crossed facing the crowd.

"You gotta give them something to look at," she stated as she would eye a new mark and coyly smile, luring him over. She did this at every bar they went to and had a line of men and free drinks at every one. By the end of the night, Rodney was shaking his head in disbelief at her abilities. Jeanie had a stack of business cards in hand from a night of potential suitors. Leigh and Rodney had to wedge her off her perch. She was a little taller than Rodney and Leigh and started to sway in her new heels. They had to each take a side with her arm over a shoulder to her left and right. She had had too many free drinks. Between the two of them, they dragged her back to the car, feet dragging behind, returning to their mother's condo. They tucked her in bed, and Leigh and Rodney slept on the sofa.

The next morning, her mother, Leigh, and Rodney were having coffee talking about their adventure when the heard Jeanie start to stir.

"Oh, my head" she moaned." Oh, my shoes! My new shoes!" They had gotten her home safely, but her shoes did not fare so well.

Worse was another date. Months later, Rodney convinced Leigh to go have a few drinks over at the Greenville Tavern and Grill. She basically just watched him drink, expecting the worst. He kept throwing them back. Now he wanted to take her to a pool hall, a little bit further up Greenville, where his ex-girlfriend works. That she should meet the girl he was engaged to. The one who he would make fun of for having fake breasts you could bounce off a wall. The one who cut open his brow, with the diamond engagement ring he bought her, during one of their fights. They had physical brawl's apparently.

Leigh drove him there but declined to go inside. Instead, she thought it was safer staying in the car. He staggered in and, about an hour later, staggered out even more intoxicated than before. As he came to get into the car, a truck was circling, wanting to park. The guy in the truck saw that Leigh was going to leave and nods to her. She gestured to him, nodding that she was leaving her parking spot. Rodney sees her nod to this guy, thinking something else. What was she doing with him while he was inside? He jumped out of the car and started yelling at the guy who is driving a standard. The guy lifted his hands, trying to explain he was just wanting to park, but his vehicle starts to roll back a little and runs over Rodney's foot. Rodney started screaming more, even louder as Leigh watches in disbelief from her car. Someone called the cops. The cops came. An ambulance came. Rodney was still screaming, cursing at everybody and everything. The police question the guy. The police questioned Leigh and asked if she was with Rodney, to come over next to him, but when she does, he starts screaming again, so the cops excuse her to go, as well as the unsuspecting guy. Rodney gets to take a ride in the ambulance, and Leigh gets to go home. Rodney was on crutches for weeks and got absolutely no sympathy from Leigh. It was his own horrible behavior.

It was a while before he would talk her into a night out again. She would resist any one on one dates, but they would go out to eat with the girls. They seemed to keep him from going out of bounds. They would hang out at Leigh's house afterward. Rodney liked to make Martinis and sit in the front yard and watch the neighbors watching him. He thought sitting watching television was the best thing, but Leigh had too much to do. On occasion, he would watch the girls. It was a help, but she couldn't really get comfortable with him before he would have another episode. He started to get snippy with Jane. Leigh started to try to spend as little time with him as possible, but still needed some help juggling her school requirements. She had started an internship at a television station for credit toward her degree, hoping it would work into a job after graduation.

At the station, they made fun of her boyfriend. He drove an old ratty truck and had bad teeth. He looked like Jed from the Hillbillies according to one of the Producers she worked for. She did well at the station, and they kept her around for a couple semesters. She did everything they would let her, from going out on shoots to pulling feeds, running scripts and manning the news desk. Her girls would see her in the background on television during the newscasts. It was cool, and Rodney made it possible for her to be at the station until one memorable night. Leigh heard news come over the wire about an automobile accident and was notified that her girls were in the vehicle. She froze for about 20 minutes in shock. She drove off to the scene and found them safe at a nearby Denny's. Rodney had flipped the truck with them in the cab as it rolled over. They were terrified. Leigh was in a state of disbelief.

Afterward, Jane told her mother how the situation had occurred. Rodney had offered to set up sound for Leigh's Video Department's festival at the university. He had access to a board and all the required equipment. He had taken the girls and went to pick up the trailer with all of the sound equipment from a friend of his. This same friend used to own the truck Rodney was driving and told Rodney that he couldn't pull the trailer with that truck. His friend had tried to do it before, and the truck flipped. His friend even begged Rodney that if he was going to do it anyway, to leave the girls, that it was too dangerous. Rodney did it anyway, knowingly endangering the children. Rodney denied what

Jane had told her mother. She could not have made up such a story and had no reason to. This brought things to a head and everything was happening all at once, total chaos. He failed her when she needed him the most. He almost killed her children.

Determination got Leigh through graduation, and her sisters all came. It was a great night that he couldn't spoil. Her mother was so proud. Rodney had now met her entire family and now made a grand gesture to Leigh. He asked her to marry him. She politely declined. But he had expected a different response and told his mother about his plans. Now his mother was expecting them to come over to her house for Christmas, to meet the girls. Rodney wouldn't let Leigh out of the Christmas at his mother's. It was beyond uncomfortable. His mother gave Leigh a Tupperware bowl full of chili for her Christmas gift. Leigh never cared for chili. Leigh found a little solace in a private joke between her and Rodney, at his mother's expense, wondering if his mother knew that Rodney liked to have sex in his mother's bed.

The very last time Leigh and Rodney went out, she was determined to break up with him and planned to drop him off at his mother's. He had stopped renting a place with his friend and kept trying to move in with Leigh, but she wouldn't have it, so he was flopping at his mother's thinking he would change Leigh's mind. Leigh had a vivid dream of walking up to a black horse and wrought iron carriage that had little bells suspended all around it that jingled as it made its way through the high grass in a little, forgotten cemetery that she had once visited. In the dream, she went up to the carriage and the grim reaper reaches down his bare-boned hand to help her climb aboard, taking a step up, she turns back, looking back down across the tombstones, saying "No, not yet. I still have too much to do," and steps back down, walking down the hill of graves. The next evening, Leigh and Rodney went out to Greenville Tavern and Grill in her car. This woman that neither knew kept telling Rodney not to leave Leigh, that it wasn't safe for her. That she would get killed. She kept pleading with him, and he kept pushing her away. She told Leigh not to leave Rodney, to stay with him. She pestered Rodney so much, they ended up leaving as soon as they finished one drink.

Leigh was determined to end their relationship and as the night wore, so did his temperament, as he became aware of her plans. She hated to fight and resisted it, especially in public. He was oblivious and waring, mercurial and full of spite. The alcohol intensified the ugliness. She did as she had planned and dropped him hollering, cursing loudly at his mother's, waking the whole house. They saw that neither should be driving and attempted to have Leigh stay, but she had not been a welcomed guest and could not stay.

In the late hours and haze of alcohol, Leigh was disoriented and became lost trying to find her way home. She ended up in Deep Elum at an underground bridge covered in graffiti and passed out behind the wheel. She felt something pushing her down into the driver's seat. There was a loud screeching sound, pounding of metal hitting concrete, twisting the vehicle as it was torn open and the passenger side wheel ripped through the floorboard, grazing her left ear, bouncing into the back seat, almost decapitating her. It would have if she had not been pushed down by some force. Immediately awake and aware, she sat up and tried to start the car. Looking around, she realized what had happened. She got

out of the car to see the damage. The passenger side wheel well was crushed into the old cement bridge. She heard some men hollering to her and turned to see a truck with half a dozen men jumping out of the back to see what had happened, asking if she was okay, if she needed their help. From a distance was the sound of sirens. As it grew louder, the guys scattered back into the truck and sped off as the police arrived. Leigh was in tears and shock. The police called a wrecker and let her call someone to come and get her. She did not know anyone other than Rodney who could find her there. Rodney did not come, but his mother's new husband did. He was kind enough to drive Leigh all the way back to her mother's home in silence. She had demolished her car and her relationship, barely surviving. Her mother had been beyond worried. She often compared her daughter to a brother she had lost just shy of being 30. The two were so similar, both loners with no real ability to connect, to trust, unconsciously being attracted to the wrong types to maintain a solitude as a self-inflicted loneliness of guilt. Leigh's only saving grace was her children.

It was done. The station had offered Leigh a job to work overnights as a Production Assistant for a pay she could not live on. She didn't know how she could work overnights. She had trouble finding child care on weekends. She could not leave her girls at night. They were too young, and it was too little to survive on. She picked up an occasional freelance offering from the station, but it was not enough and not reliable. She picked up other Production Assistant work but it was just temporary. Most production gigs wouldn't hire her because she had children. They wanted workers with more flexibility than she could manage. After all that struggle, hard work, and debt to get a Bachelor's degree, she could not find regular work. She freelanced for a year and decided to try to go back to school. Her girls were not yet old enough to be left unattended, and this would buy them some more time and Leigh more debt.

Rodney had been involved in Parrot Joe's as a Manager of his brother's restaurant that was selling cocaine out the back door. They ended up being forced to shutter their doors for tax evasion. Rodney had gone back to repairing cars at a local garage. It galled him to be a blue-collar worker with dirty hands.

Leigh had to move forward. She couldn't find employment that would pay the mortgage, so she took a few steps back and enrolled back in school. She had hoped her situation would have improved, but it had not. She had to somehow get through the next few years until the girls were old enough to be left after school at home alone. She was accepted into the Master's program for Radio, Television, and Film at a university in North Texas, but the hour drive there and back was too difficult to be able to take care of the girls and their needs effectively. Furthermore, the philosophy of the school administration was not conducive to a single parents' struggles. It was a curious prejudice that Leigh was faced with. If she doesn't have a husband, she doesn't deserve to do better. She's not like a normal family. She had even been told throughout the years by various teachers, other women, a backhanded insult. "Your kids seem so normal, you wouldn't know they came from a single parent household." Leigh could never knowingly make a vow that she could not keep. It was better for her and her girls not to have the bad behavior of a bad relationship, addictions, all of the things she had witnessed as a child, be a part of her own children's lives. Wasn't it a parent's primary goal to put the children's needs before her own, to protect them and teach them to be a part of the greater good? But it became a question of their nature versus her nurture, depending upon the individual and how impacting either can be.

She ran into an old classmate from her former university who was transferring to a private university and how it was so much closer to home, such a better university. It was and it was even more expensive, even more debt, but it was all she could manage to be able to be closer to her children, to be more available to their needs. She made the transfer and the transition worked well for all of their needs. She graduated with a Master's in Radio, Television, and Film, and Jane was almost 12 and Marie was almost 9.

It was a rare occasion, but Leigh and Jeanie would attempt a night out. They had very different objectives and approaches but it chased away the blues. Jeanie liked to be trendy and the latest trend was all things cowboy. Leigh was more of the artist type, all in black. This evening, Jeanie was calling the shots. They were to meet at a little, new honky-tonk that had just opened up. As usual, Jeanie was late. Leigh was watching for her at the bar, when a portly man approached. He has on a cowboy hat, to cover his bald spot and a huge belt buckle to draw attention to his penis, but it just emphasized how fat he was, digging into his gut. He saunters up to her, asks what she's drinking, and buys her a shot of tequila. "Cheers...you look like you belong in Deep Elum."

Leigh spots Jeanie's arrival as very timely. She pardons the gentleman to make her way in a crowded, elbow to elbow, field of yee-haws. She stops next to a booth filled with half a dozen patrons, seated boy, girl, boy girl and attempts to talk to Jeanie. Jeanie spots a girlfriend, Crystal and asks Leigh to wait while she went to round her up.

Leigh waited for Jeanie, but a woman in the booth behind her hollered up to Leigh "Is that all your real hair?" having very long, thick red hair, Leigh responds with a hand across her lower abdominal, "No, I have a little more here!" The guy on the very end of the booth heard her well, his mouth now agape as his date could be heard "Whaddid she say?, Whaddid she say?" Leigh leaves and goes out alone to Dallas to listen to some live music.

Jeanie and her girlfriend Crystal had similar approaches, and it was a curious thing to watch the two compete in their expeditions and exhibition. Crystal was a very tall, horsefaced model who was all about what money they had and how she could benefit kind of girl. She would date someone and never tell them she had a daughter. The two together were a significant threat to the wellbeing of the male populace in the Dallas-Fort Worth region. They knew mutual acquaintances having a soiree, a costumed affair at a large estate on the local Lake for Halloween. Leigh was invited to tag along. She met up with Jeanie at her apartment, knowing that Jeanie was still not ready. Jeanie got dressed, full makeup just to go to the mailbox. Leigh is dressed, of course, all in black suede as Zorro with a whip. Jeanie is a Vampiress in a black long negligee with ample, bolstered cleavage, accentuating her accouterments and attraction. Crystal arrives as Jeanie is just ready to go. She saw Crystal in her belly dancer attire, bare midriff, and turns back, making them wait as she makes an adjustment. Jeanie turns her lingerie around backward for a more plunging cleavage, almost to her navel, and is now ready to go!

Sure enough, they had stopped to pick up some beer ahead of time, not knowing what to expect and with a beer each in hand, they stuffed the 18 pack into the bushes. They walked in and all of the guests had drunk all of the beer at the party and were down to the hard stuff. The girls were instantly popular, having a beer in their hand. Ok, forget the outfits, it's about the beer. Leigh made one friend sharing her beer, as Jeanie and Crystal mixed in to see who was there. There were some older gentlemen whom Leigh was able to chat with. One of these gentlemen owned a local football team that was talking about moving his team, building a new stadium. He asked Leigh if she would like to be a part of their dancing group that met up out in another local town a few times a month. He asked to meet with her a few days later. He was married and a lot older. She told him what he wanted to hear but wasn't up to the whole sneaking married men thing. Jeanie and Crystal became bored, no action they wanted, not knowing who was actually there.

Leigh had gotten a job with a telephone company during a job fair. It was a stable income that was a Monday through Friday, operator, computer job with benefits. She went through training, and once they were set up in their new facility, the employer was mandating all new hires had to work Saturdays. Leigh refused and was fired as a result. She ended up getting a telemarketing job with a real estate relocation company for a year.

She had made a few friends and started to spend a little time with one of her co-workers who had recently been divorced, Angela. She had been married since she was 18, and now with two teenage boys at home, she was wanting a night out to prowl. It was always a challenge to balance your parental needs with your adult needs as a single mother. It had been a while since Leigh had gone out, and she was overdue.

The two women succeeded in finding accommodating company. The impetus had been directed for Angela's coupling attempts. Leigh did what she could to be a supportive friend. Angela used her a bait, to lure in what she wanted to catch. One early night out, the girls had gone downtown to a sports bar. Angela would let Leigh know who she had eyes for. One, in particular, had interests in Leigh instead. As an effort to let Angela succeed, Leigh would politely excuse herself from the two, walking across the loud bar, to the doorman, trying to make conversation and give her girlfriend more leverage for her new interest. With beer in hand, she passed a table of men going back and forth. They kept raising their beers and hollering as she passed. Unbeknownst to Leigh, the doorman had put a sign on Leigh's back "will trade dress for beer. " Everyone roared once Leigh realized that she was the entertainment.

On another similar, after work venture, the two went to lower Greenville. Leigh visited old haunts from her time with

Rodney. One of these bars had a balcony, and some men were calling down to Leigh and Angela about wanting to give piggyback rides around the rooftop. A spark of fun gleamed in Angela. The two went up to check out the beckoning men. They pulled up a table, but the service on the rooftop was subpar. There were 3 men. Angela liked the youngest one, and the fat one liked Leigh. Leigh did not really mind. It was just some fun, nothing serious. Needing drinks, it was time to abandon the balcony and find service downstairs. The heavyset one with big thick glasses, Jose offered to give Leigh a piggyback ride. He carried her like a little stuffed animal on his back, down the stairs. They all sat around a table, with Angela playing footsies under the table. Again, the one she eyed, eyed Leigh, so Leigh pulled back and paid attention to the unwanted Jose. As it turned out, the heavy-set guy was the local Manager at a large corporation entertaining two out of town Managers from California. Angela was very forward, and the younger one was very obliging. She glowed with the attention. Everyone went back to Jose's apartment. Angela went off with Mr. California, while Leigh played nice with the other two. Everyone had drinks, and Leigh had to find her girlfriend. Jose wanted to see more of Leigh after the California guys went back home. Angela had fun, but they never called her back. Leigh had made a new friend.

Leigh and Jose dated for about six months, but their affiliation was short-lived, not serious for Leigh. At the referral of her oldest sister, Julie, Leigh got a job as a Personal Lines Appraiser with an international insurance company. The insurance company required her to move to Tulsa and put her through training for a few weeks. She rented their little home, rented a large moving van, and piled up her household herself. With the family dog in her lap, she drove the biggest truck she had ever driven from the DallasFort Worth region to Tulsa. She managed to find a duplex in a good school system and got her girls registered for a new school system. She had to have her mother come and stay with the girls, while she was sent up to New Jersey. This was the first time she had to be away from her children, and it was so difficult for everyone. They had been in the same schools, same home for 9 years, leaving her mother behind and trying to become as independent and responsible as she could.

The new job kept Leigh on the road, and Jane began to get into mischief. They enjoyed the money the new job created, but the dynamics of the family were changing. Jane became sexually active at 13. She was starting to experiment with drugs and challenging her mother's authority. Leigh had no support system. Her mother was back in Texas, but soon she would be too. Her employer transferred her back to where they had just moved from 10 months before, back to Texas. They provided a relocation package, and she was able to buy another home, a larger home so that the girls could have their own rooms and a little privacy as teenagers.

Leigh did what she could to try to keep her girls in line, but Jane was not going to abide by anyone or anything. She had been an honor student, took violin for years, but now she wanted to be the dominant female. She began to fight with her mother at every turn. Trying to keep things together at work was difficult too. She had tried to meet up with her former friend, Jose. They had kept in touch while Leigh was in

Tulsa, but he never made a visit. He seemed to make promises, but not follow through.

Now Leigh was back in town, and Jose invited her over. He had another co-worker at his apartment and they had been drinking margaritas. Jose offered Leigh a margarita, and Jose's friend decided to leave. Alone after over a year away, Jose began to tell Leigh how upset he had become about her just up and leaving, moving to Tulsa like she did, and now she wasn't going anywhere. This was in an unfamiliar tone. Leigh sensed hatefulness, and Jose was acting very strangely. She had just had a couple of sips of her drink, but he kept trying to refill it. His tone and manner had darkened. Leigh became afraid. He reached at her, grabbing her shirt at the neckline forcefully. She tugged backwards, breaking free; she ran out of his apartment. Halfway home, she was dizzy and unclear. She was pulled over by a police officer. She couldn't understand what was going on. She had just had less than one drink. She was handcuffed and incarcerated for driving under the influence of alcohol. She called her sister Debbie, but her sister refused to come and get her out of jail. It wasn't even 9 o'clock in the evening. Her sister believed the worst in Leigh, that she had drunk too much and deserved to stay in jail overnight. Leigh was stripped and searched, not understanding how she was so out of it. The jailer thought she was on drugs. She was but not knowingly. She even tried calling Jose, but he wouldn't respond to her. It was so odd. Even after her sister, Debbie finally showed up around noon the next day. None of it made any sense. Furthermore, no one believed her. She was charged with DWI, driving while intoxicated. She was convicted and put on probation. She was allowed a permit to drive for work purposes only. Her mother was ashamed, and now her work was alerted. She had to drive as part of her job.

She had to get a second job to be able to pay for all of the ensuing costs of an attorney and fines. She got an overnight job, stocking shelves at a grocery store to pay for her penance, troubles. Sleep was not something she could afford. She had to do this for about six months.

The misdemeanor charge put Leigh's job in jeopardy. Now Leigh had never dated co-workers. She was uncomfortable with that line and kept her adult life private. The insurance company would require after-hours work functions, dinners, and encouraged co-workers to drink together. One of the chief appraisers in the Dallas office prided himself on how many co-workers he had bagged, like notches on his gun handle. He had his sights set on Leigh. She ignored him as much as she could, but now he was her supervisor and the whole crew was meeting down in Houston. Some drove down in the company cars, some flew depending upon their work schedule but all had bets on who would do who, being a new kid to the come-hither game.

Leigh hung out with everyone, had dinner, and went to a local watering hole. She had been operating with very little sleep working overnights stocking shelves, so she was wide awake as the others dropped out one by one. She had hitched a ride back to where they were staying, and it was down to her and her supervisor. It was almost 3 in the morning. He gave in and drove them back to the hotel.

The crew had a morning meeting at 7. Everyone was anxious to see what had happened from the night before. Leigh was on time, but her supervisor was worse for the ware, disheveled and bleary-eyed. He had lost his bet and did not bag another one. Leigh tried to make light of it, but it became an issue.

Chapter 5. Disbarred Felon Huston

Leigh did not give in and lost her job despite her best efforts to hang on. She was pushed out. She had tried to find work, but with a DWI, no one would hire her. She decided to dust off her Real Estate license and go back to selling on straight commission. She had maintained her educational requirements and now interviewed with one of the Brokerages she had previously worked for. She started working on making money, but her new Manager, Joan, was a very biased, jealous woman. She had a weight problem and was grossly obese. She treated the Agents unfavorably. Those who worked for her depended upon how they sided with her in a mutually gluttonous approach or otherwise. Her office of over 75 Agents, mostly women were known for having the heaviest Agents around. It was like growing up in a house of all girls all over again, too much estrogen. Joan required office tours of new listings. Having to get into a crowded car with a bunch of menstruating women was cruel. Leigh had yet another discriminatory situation to be faced with, but the office was close to home and Leigh knew the area well.

Joan's' office Agents crowded every real estate luncheon as the joke of all of the Brokerages. At these functions, Leigh was able to network with other Agents from other offices. While working her way through a lunch line in reverse, having dessert first was the only way she was able to get any food before it was all gone. She caught the attention of another Agent, Ed. He was from a competing Brokerage who found humor in Leigh's ability to work around the situation. The two started to meet up at real estate event, comparing notes and issues of the business. Leigh had found a muchneeded friend.

Back at the office, Joan would make Leigh attend new Agent meetings, regardless of the fact she had been licensed for 15 years and had extensive experience with Real Estate, working for builders, and appraising high-end homes. Joan stated in front of a room full of new Agents to Leigh that, "It takes more than just being cute and funny to make it in this business," and that was why Joan never worked on straight commission. She was an administrator. She ran an office and played politics over who showed her the most love. Leigh was not able to accommodate her and was able to attract business without her help. Joan had her favorites who would report to her. She would reward them with referrals. They were fed leads by her and would become dependent upon her to give them business. Leigh had to find her own clients and put her knowledge and formal education to use. She created advertising on a local cable channel, postcards, mailers, and began marketing herself. The more successful she became; the more Joan became disparagingly ugly toward her. Joan's underlings would accuse Leigh of stealing leads, office supplies, anything Joan could blame on her, none of which Leigh had committed. Leigh began setting up her home office to avoid these accusations. It became very apparent that Leigh was unwelcomed. Leigh would pull little antics, to set Joan on edge. She would take a stack of Joan's business cards and give them out to unsuspecting men at a bar, acting like she was Joan and ask the selected victim to "give her a call for lunch or drinks", so Joan would get calls from strange men wanting to take her out. It took her a little bit to figure it out.

Leigh had trouble from all sides. The more money she made, the more trouble Jane would get into. Leigh started listing homes for a local builder and working weekends. Jane started stealing, pawning everything in their home to pay for her drug-induced state of fun. Leigh was on edge in her own home. While she was working, her daughter, Jane, would have junior criminals parade in and out with whatever they could make a few dollars on. Leigh never had much, but they would take anything. Jane, would climb out an upstairs window at night or sneak her little minions in. Leigh kept a loaded gun and would try to stop their coming and going, but to no avail. This made the drug-induced Jane paranoid that her mother would shoot her own daughter.

During the height of her bad behavior, their father had yet again stopped paying child support, and the State's Attorney General's office called Leigh and Jamey back to court. It was a familiar process, but with a new glitch. Jamey claimed he wanted to start visiting the girls. After court, he and his, then current, wife wanted to come by the house. He had been raising the wife's daughters and had nothing to do with his own. He had not seen the girls since they thought he was a roofer at the ages of 2 and 5. Jane was now 16 and Marie was 13. Being an ass, neither accepted him, but Jane wanted to get into his pocket, and the two drug users conspired. Jane claimed that her mother had pointed her gun at her. This never happened.

Jamey used this in court. He had promised Jane a car if she would collude, come and live with him, and pull everyone back in court. Then, he would make Leigh pay him child support. He did this. She did this. Everyone went back to court, and the Judge told Jamey, "Wait, you have two children together. You will have custody of one and she has custody of the other now so no one pays support.

"Jamey turned so red, he seemed to actually steam with anger and rage. Jane began living the drug-strewn life in an East Texas trailer, doing whatever she pleased, unsupervised. Her father traveled and was never home. It was not a fancy doublewide. It was a run-down tin box. He did keep it tidy, but it was over 20 years old. She would steal his cocaine stash and replace it with flour. This would make him mad. When they were out of flour, Jane replaced it with baking soda. She was angry with her father. She would take condoms and spit in them, putting them under her father's pillow, so Jamey would find them after he got home from being on the road, thinking his wife was entertaining other men while he was away. Jane was a contributing cause of their divorce. He wanted custody and got a little comeuppance as a result. She was a lot like her father. He got custody of Jane, and she never got a car, instead, during his watch, she got pregnant at 16. Now he didn't want her, and Leigh had to take him back to court and reverse custody.

Jane came back home pregnant and proud. She went back to her high school, refusing to stand down. Her grades were too high; she excelled despite her situation. The high school, couldn't make her hide in an alternative school and the example she was setting wasn't pretty to witness. She was due the same day as her graduation. Her classmates were taking bets on her going into labor on stage during the ceremony. She wanted that also, but she only made it through the rehearsal. She ended up going into labor the day before. What a monster she had become. Maybe Rodney had been right. Leigh had developed an uncomfortable reaction to having her daughter in her home. She could not be trusted. She stole whatever she could lay her hands on. She was so smart, but so bad. She was becoming a criminal, and Leigh could not stop her. Jane knew the difference between right and wrong, but it did not matter. All of this took place as the youngest daughter, Marie watched. Marie was hurt that her father made no notice of her. Leigh did what she could to try to assuage the situation for Marie, to reward her for being good.

Leigh had started to have a little extra income and would partake in furniture auctions. She had never had much, and now they had a little bigger home to spread around in that echoed from the emptiness. The auctions were like gambling but you had something to show for it. She had invited her new Agent friend Ed along. The two enjoyed these breaks from the crazy life on straight commission. Ed had been in the same part of Texas since childhood. Having been raised locally, he was very aware of who was who and had spotted one of these notables at an auction one evening. This notable was more notorious for his bad behavior, having been from a prominent local family, he had been disbarred as an attorney but the reasons were not clear. Leigh had recalled his real estate achievements with various commercial developments and buildings from two decades prior. He was a curiosity to her. Huston was a portly man, 16 years her senior. He was very unkempt. He was a little taller than Leigh and very broad, with piercing blue eyes behind his thick-framed glasses. He had foul manors, talking with food in his mouth, spitting bits out at whomever had ventured too close, but he was very knowledgeable about Real Estate. She thought she could learn something from him.

Ed was excited about the encounter. He acted as though it was interacting with royalty. Leigh introduced herself to Huston as Ed watched from a safe distance. Huston was very skittish, disappearing in the audience. He would work through the crowd and interject comments to her throughout the rest of the evening. Ed suggested that Leigh invite Huston to meet with them later. In doing so, Huston did not seem sure about meeting the two afterward. Ed and Leigh went ahead as planned, arriving at the designated restaurant. Sure enough, Huston made an appearance. He was very reclusive. This was highly uncommon for him. He was shy with the uninvited attention that Leigh and Ed had shown him. Huston glared indirectly at Leigh as Ed was amused. Huston was interested in Leigh, and you could see him devising thoughts that were undisclosed, being coy. Huston was very unlike anyone Leigh had met. He was highly intelligent, highly educated, and had completely fallen from grace.

Huston was a very confident, conceited, prejudice man from a very privileged family. He felt like he was far better than

Leigh. She should be thankful for his association, after all, if it were not for his prison stint, he would have been the Governor of Texas. He paraded around naked with his chest out, sucking in his gut completely unaware of how unattractive he was in his egotistical vanity. His sexual initiative was self-serving. He had no care to be mutually pleasuring. He was more talkative than active, very unkempt and ungroomed. He likes body odor and enjoyed his own. Leigh was very sensitive, being very fair. She developed allergies to his lack of hygiene, which undermined any trust she could have for him.

Huston began calling on Leigh, but in very controlled situations. Huston did not want her to know anything about him unless he first put a spin on whatever it was. He would only meet her in private at her house. Leigh had already researched his background, but let him take the lead in his disclosures, in his presentations of fact as to his background and who he was. She knew he had been disbarred but did not know why. According to him, it was as a result of an old nemesis he had, Stan, who owned some commercial properties and was a licensed Real Estate Broker that Leigh actually had known. She had worked for him years ago at the gift shop when she was 16.

Leigh knew of Huston's commercial properties. He had constructed a high-rise on the corner of the interstate that was a landmark. It was by far the most appealing high-rise in town. During the construction, Huston had borrowed federal funds, but had been juggling his moneys, co-mingling, which was illegal in Texas. According to Huston, the bridge across the interstate was untimely demolished and kept under construction with constant delays keeping it from being completed. The construction was intentionally being held up by his old buddy Stan, so Huston could not get his new building pre-leased to alleviate mounting expenses. The contract for constructing this building included a fountain in the center of the circular drive. Huston claimed he ran out of money and had neglected to have the fountain constructed, violating the contract. He was sued in court, and when found guilty, he surrendered his law license and served one year as a convicted felon in a federal prison. Stan proceeded to take over the building and parcel off many of the attractions it held, stripping it of its attractiveness, and desirability, raping Huston's masterpiece. Leigh knew Stan, and he seemed very capable of such contrived atrocities if crossed into his business. He and his wife Jan were very vain and very monetary. She recalled seeing Huston's billboards, trying to lease the building 2 decades prior. Huston had found the sympathy others had denied him in Leigh.

They began seeing each other, but Huston wanted total control over Leigh's interactions. That wasn't possible. Leigh had too many other commitments, and Huston would become angry, frustrated with his lack of control. Huston thought he could step into Leigh's family and curtail her children's need for a father figure. Jane would not have it. She referred to Huston with his new moniker, Hucifer. It became a war zone in every way. Marie did not want to share her mother either and would intentionally create problems to pull Leigh back from Huston's influence. The nightmare intensified in a multi-faceted and highly charged state of turmoil. There was no peace at home and no peace at work.

Leigh found sanctuary staying busy, having real estate functions, open houses, filling her weekends, her time to avoid the ensuing battles. It was relentless. Marie had started venturing into her own type of trouble with a boy from school. He was as obliging as she wanted him to be. It was something she had control over, someone she could get to do what she wanted. Huston and Leigh tried to hinder Marie's adventures into drugs and alternative behaviors. Marie was getting into troubles that pulled Mother back into the fray.

Many things were in flux. Leigh's mother had sold her condominium and moved out to Georgia. She had been a part of Leigh's little family dynamics from the start but was now wanting to see the rest of her grandchildren. Four of Leigh's sisters were living in Georgia and Florida. The had promised to rotate their mother around between them, but she ended up staying at Julie's, living in her basement apartment, a room with no windows. None of the sisters took the time to include her in their busy lives. As their mother's eyesight was failing, the more dangerous her driving became, and no one seemed to notice or even try to curtail her problems. Leigh began flying back to Georgia to see her mother who had developed colon cancer. Her mother's treatment, chemotherapy, had made her weak and her skin was sallow. She was smaller than Leigh had recalled. She had some good days and some not so good days.

On one of these trips, Leigh drove out with Huston. Jeanie had been driving up from Florida and asked if she could stay at the hotel that Leigh and Huston were staying at, to help counterbalance the expense. Leigh agreed. Huston wanted to try the local pork barbeque as his motivation for the trip. He was always motivated by food. For the first six months he was dating Leigh, he did not know she could cook. Unlike Huston, Leigh took care of herself, working out and staying in shape, so he just assumed she could not cook, that skinny people can't cook. He had very strange prejudices and beliefs. He would always try to come up with little pet names for Leigh until she pointed out that they were always food related and that there was something very wrong with her heavy-set boyfriend referring to her as food. Jeanie knew of Huston but had never met him before. Leigh tried to prepare Huston for the event, that she would probably hit on him, she likes the attention, but he was still unaware.

In the hotel room, early their first morning, Leigh and Huston shared one bed, and Jeanie had the other. Jeanie had just gotten into her robe while Leigh was getting ready, taking a shower for the day ahead. Jeanie barges into the bath, pulling back the shower curtain, as to inspect Leigh naked in the shower. Leigh just shakes her head, laughing at her sibling. Huston is still tucked in bed. Jeanie in just her robe, eyes Huston, making her way over to him as he fakes being asleep, playing opossum. She sits at his side leaning over his face with her breasts exposed, dangling them, her pendulous boobs over him just as Leigh comes out of the shower to see as Huston fearfully pulling the covers over his head trying to avoid Jeanie and any potential misconstrued perception of the situation. Leigh just laughs as she continues to get ready. Huston was without words. This was a first.

Back at home, Marie had gotten caught at school smoking.

Leigh did not condone smoking and prohibited it as a parent. Marie bought her cigarettes without her mother's consent but now a court says Leigh is responsible to pay a fine as a result of her minor daughter's behavior that she tried to curtail. Marie should be responsible for her own bad behavior. She did this on her own and the Judge agreed. Marie had to work off her fine with community service. This actually had a positive influence on her. Furthermore, Leigh sought to have Marie spend her Sundays at Huston's mother's while Leigh had to work as a way to keep her from any more out of bounds behavior. This relationship made a difference in Marie. Huston's mother taught Marie to knit, and the two became good friends.

Years ago, Huston's father and sister had died. It was just him and his mother, and theirs was a very strained relationship. Huston had been passed off to his grandmother with the arrival of his baby sister when he was about 2. He had never really resolved his early separation anxieties, but he did want an heir, someone to pass on his family's name and wealth. They had been in that Texas town for over 100 years. His uncle had been a state Senator who lived in Corsicana as a rancher. Huston had been stripped of any money and any ability to earn money with his conviction. The government held a judgment over him from that conviction for over a million dollars. It was a very deep hole, and he was waiting it out, to fall off of his credit to be able to move forward with his life. He could not have anything in his name without it being attached as part of that debt. Even his home had been put in his sister's name, but that had to change. She had died.

It was ruled suicide but that may not have been the case. Huston believed there had been foul play and that his brother-in-law, Jeff, had been the perpetrator. It had never been proven, and now Huston had to confront Jeff to get him to sign over his own home, the remainder of his sister's estate and put it into his Uncles name.

Leigh was to be Huston's accomplice to achieve this. They set up a date with Jeff to go down to Austin, to get his signatures on the required documents. Huston was worried that Jeff would claim Huston's house in the settlement so they needed to act quickly, especially since Jeff was down to the last monies of the sister's estate. Jeff was a leathered-faced, stringy-haired Mason who lived with a new girlfriend in a little place just on the fringe of Austin. Both worked at a local hospital. Jeff was a janitor who cleaned up after operations, any type of blood and guts mess. He was very creepy. He had a room filled with Nazi and Mason memorabilia. He did not seem to mesh with what Huston had described his sister to have been. She was a doctor of Psychology who studied sleep disorders. Nothing connected properly. After an overnight stay, Huston and Leigh had gotten more than they had wanted. Huston was able to keep his home now in his Uncle's name.

Huston was wanting to convince Leigh to abide by his wishes despite what she wanted. He encouraged her to take the test to become a Broker and start her own business. This they agreed, and she proceeded, starting her own Brokerage. Huston wanted her to have another baby. This was not something she could even imagine. He had an assortment of odd jobs for minimal income. He would throw a lawnmower in the back of his old sedan and mow the yards of family friends. He would buy antiques at auctions and try to resell them at retail malls. He was running machine parts for his friend, Stephen, who was the supplier for a manufacturer.

Huston would take payments and make deposits into a bank account on Stephen's behalf. He had also been making withdrawals from that same account with a forged signature by befriending a couple of the tellers. When Stephen, finally found out, Huston was still able to convince the friend to maintain their relationship. Huston was talented at manipulation and persuasion. Sometimes, you just see what you want to see.

Huston had a creative approach and would spend hours devising a plan for someone else's demise. He tried to convince Leigh to approach a property owner to sell her trailer park, so that Huston could resell it and convert it into a more lucrative parcel by lying to her about the initial intent to gain her trust and willingness. Leigh couldn't pretend that she could go along with such contrived behavior. Huston was always working on some plan, some scheme through anyone he could to make himself undeclared money. He had no ethics, and now she discovered he had no morals either.

Huston's mother had purchased some sewing items from an international auction house in London, so she agreed to fund a trip for Huston to pick them up. Huston included Leigh as his stowaway at his mother's expense. Leigh had gotten her passport ahead of time but it was a last-minute scramble to Austin for Huston's passport replacement, being unable to locate it during the final hours prior. He would always seem to be missing something despite all of his preplanning and preparation. Huston and Leigh flew into Bristol and got a rental car. It was a manual shift that Huston couldn't drive, but Leigh could and drove them all over the southern countryside. She wanted to take pictures and enjoy the scenery. Huston wanted to control when and what she took pictures of, and they argued constantly. He would even argue with locals about America being better than their beloved Britain. He was referred to on several occasions as an "Ugly American". It was humiliating. At one-point, Huston was upset with Leigh for being across the street taking pictures of a Church and began yelling at her, scolding her so much that a passerby asked if she was alright and if they should call the police. In every town, as the week wore on, his flare-ups intensified. The stress of the trip was too much for his civility.

Upon arriving in Bath, the two visited an antique shop. Huston was delegating to Leigh how to behave, how to pronounce Bath correctly as "Bauth". She was humiliated by his arrogance.

When Huston asked the shopkeeper to verify his pronunciation, the gentleman politely said, "You could pronounce it that way. However, we say Bath." Interacting with others at a pub, Huston did not want to disclose that the pair were staying at a hostel. He wanted to give the impression that they had money and were staying at an expensive hotel. Once again everyone saw through his guise, amazed that Leigh was with the "Ugly American". She was assumed to be a local and fit in well, making friendly conversations. This made Huston even more difficult. He left Leigh in Oxford and made the trek to London via train without her. He was so hateful. To come all that way and not even be able to see London was typical of his spitefulness, but Leigh made the best of the situation and enjoyed the stress-free time away from Huston.

Leigh had made the transition from being an Agent working for another Broker to being her own Broker on her own. She had her office set up at her home and would be in and out with work all day. On one of those hectic back and forth days, Huston was at her house without her knowledge. He had gotten on her business computer and was interacting on a pornographic site, soliciting women. He had typed up his profile, touting himself as 10 years younger, having racehorses and traveling the world, needing a female to accompany him. Leigh breezed in unannounced and printed out his profile. On one hand, he wants to marry, and have a baby, while the other hand, is busy collecting other women to entertain him in his fictional depiction of a life he may have once led. When she confronted him, he completely denied it, so she handed him his printed profile. He claimed he only was after nude pictures from his correspondence with other women. They split over this. She could not trust him. No one could trust him. He had accumulated many of his antiques in her garage, so he would not have to pay for storage. At this point, Leigh and Marie took all of his belongings and placed them in his front yard, emptying out her garage of his furniture.

Leigh had so much pressure from so many different things all at once; she sought to change. She began to go blind in one eye. Her eye was going black, not being able to see out of it due to all of the pressure. Her health was wearing down from all sides. She needed to be able to escape from everyone and everything. She would wander off with Ed to go on long drives in between the clients. She wanted to find a lake house, a second home far away to relax. After searching for years, she discovered a place on a little private lake in East Texas. It was perfect, and she proceeded to finance it as an investment towards her eventual retirement.

Jane had not slowed down. She had come home only to pick up speed in her wild existence. She had moved out to Georgia to be with Leigh's other sisters. Jane was welcome but should not have been. Leigh tried to warn them, but they believed that Jane had been subject to bad parenting. It was all Leigh's doing, poor, little Jane. This was always how each sister tried to help, and it would always end with Jane stealing and creating more problems. She ended up being sent back to Leigh, after being jailed for shoplifting with one of her boyfriends, while her daughter, Leigh's granddaughter, Ashley was with them at a mall. Jane had burned through all of her extended family's kindness and tolerance.

Jane came back home and was pregnant again. She ran off again with a boyfriend that beat her in front of Ashley. She came back again, only to become pregnant with her third child. It was head spinning and amazing that she could do so much harm, commit so much crime, do so many drugs, and still manage to get pregnant. Leigh tried to get Jane into a better situation. She was dragging those babies into one drug riddled apartment complex to another. She couldn't live at home. She stole anything anyone had to pawn it, and now she had two children and one on the way to think about. Leigh helped Jane buy a little brick home, much like the first one they had known for so many years. Jane did not appreciate something she had been set up in, having it come to her so easily. Leigh did not do it for Jane, it was for her grandchildren, but Jane never put her childrens' needs first.

Anything you bought the children, Jane pawned, and traded for drugs. She was deplorable, and her addiction took over her world. She was like her father and Leigh's mother in that regard. Addiction ran on both sides of the family.

Meanwhile, Marie had not been happy either. Leigh couldn't keep anything together outside of business it seemed. Marie had been using crack cocaine and had lost so much weight. Leigh feared for her daughter's health. At school, Marie started to exhibit suicidal tendencies, painting graphic pictures of bloody situations. The school didn't know how to respond, thus expelling her. Marie decided to run away. She ended up staying with a guy from school at his parents' house. Leigh had no idea where she had gone, being in a panic for her daughter's safety, but much like her older sister Jane, Marie created a story of her mother not caring. Leigh was a bad parent was how she spun the story to Leigh's youngest sister, Debbie. Debbie had failed Leigh again. Debbie knew where Marie was, that she was okay, but did not have the decency to tell Leigh. Furthermore, these other parents were harboring the runaway daughter. Marie came back home, but now Leigh had had enough. Leigh took Marie to her father's and left her on his doorstep. If Marie wanted to live like a druggie, have no accountability for her own behavior, that was the place. This time at Jamey' this daughter promised to go back to school. She agreed to either be in school full-time or work full-time if she was at Leigh's house. Leigh took her back. Marie finished early at an alternative school and enrolled in the University of Texas. Leigh was so proud that Marie was trying.

Trying to balance everything that was going on, Leigh was told that her mother could travel and made plans with her. Her mother wanted to see Las Vegas. Leigh bought plane tickets and booked a hotel room. Marie agreed to go and help if her grandmother had any health issues. Leigh and Marie flew out to Atlanta for Thanksgiving ready to take her mother on their planned trip. Leigh's mother was not feeling well enough. She would have episodes, but they would pass.

The following week, Leigh called to check on her mother, and she had worsened. They wanted to admit her into the hospital. Leigh threw a bag together and went back to Atlanta, now being told it would be her last visit with her mother.

Leigh arrived at the hospital. Her mother was at the end of her path. Her chemotherapy had created a weakness in her intestinal tract lining, causing sepsis. She was in a lot of pain but put on high doses of Codeine and minimally coherent. She died November 29th, 2006. Leigh returned to Texas.

At college, Marie did not enroll in Architecture and was pushed away and ignored by the department with her inquiries. Leigh tried to encourage Marie to persist, but she signed up for engineering instead. Leigh thought it was a mistake knowing she was being set up to fail, not having the strength in mathematics. It seemed like the Architectural Department was truly blocking women from their school. She did not even get through the first semester and would not show Leigh her grades. She had met a man in one of her classes, Rick Lacey. He was doing well in engineering, so she sought some help from him. She had not disclosed to her mother that she was failing and had dropped out. Leigh found out when summer semester started, and Marie still had no grades and was not signing up for classes. Marie argued that going over summer was not included in full-time. It was for Leigh when she went, and if Marie wasn't going to be school, she needed to get a job. She ignored her mother as long as she could. Leigh was not going to see her go back to drugs if she could help it and pushed for her to either get a job or move out. As it turned out, she did not finish a full semester and was not enrolled for the summer. This was not what they had agreed to. She refused to attend school or get a job at eighteen. She moved out to live with that young man, Rick she met in one of her engineering classes. He lived with his mother and stepfather in their garage apartment.

Leigh was so lost. She felt like she was completely alone, and now she was. Both of her children were on their own and out of the house, Jane with children of her own. They had been the center of Leigh's world for her whole adult life. She had always done for them and now did not know what to do. She felt like she was drifting away and needed to be grounded somehow.

6. Marital Diss Gregory

Leigh's business had really been exciting, but overwhelming with her personal life. The market was shifting and her income would too, so she sought something stable. She got a job in government, far from Huston and her girls. She moved her belongings into the lake house and rented her home. She had gotten a Property Manager job with the State of Hawaii.

It was an exciting and much-needed change. It was unbelievably hard on her dog, having to be quarantined for almost 6 months. She found an apartment in Waikiki and began her new life. She had to travel to different islands to manage properties for the state. She began digging into her new work. She often had projects that involved other departments and the State Attorney General's Office. The Attorney, Will became a regular at Leigh's office. He was a married man and was very forward to Leigh. She had to work with him, and his amorous behavior was obvious to everyone. Leigh's co-workers would tease her that her "boyfriend" was looking for her. This was very uncomfortable and unwanted.

Leigh tried to make friends with the other women at work, one in particular, Lori, wanted to go out for drinks. She had been divorced for several years, but her ex-husband had recently died, and she was needing someone in her life. The two women agreed to meet at Leigh's and go out in Waikiki, but Lori never called and never showed up. At work, Lori did not mention her behavior, not having the courtesy to follow through. Leigh decided to check out a local auction house and invited Lori along. If she was a no-show, Leigh would still be able to have an enjoyable outing. Lori made it to this event and even made a few purchases, but there were really no prospective, available men. Leigh decided to have an evening out on her own and scout around for a place that they could meet. She found a local sports bar in walking distance from her apartment. It was crowded with men. At the bar, Leigh ordered a drink and sitting on the corner stool, a tall, greying man with blue eyes turned to her. He smiled and offered to move down to give her his seat. Gregory had a heavy New England accent and was watching the Patriots play football. The two talked about sports. He asked if she would meet up with him the next evening for dinner. She responded with, "Sure, why not?"

Back at work, Leigh talked to Lori about this sports bar and Lori agreed to check it out that coming weekend. That evening, Leigh went back to meet Gregory for dinner. He was there, but apparently had forgotten about their plans. The two had some drinks and decided to take a walk on the beach. She told Gregory about Lori, so they invited a friend of Gregory's to join them with another as a blind date for Lori. That weekend the guy was a no-show, so the three went out to dinner together. Lori was indecisive and whined. She wasn't going to enjoy the evening no matter where they went, so the evening ended early. Gregory wanted to continue seeing Leigh. He was staying in Honolulu just across the Ala Wai in some condominiums his company provided. He was only there temporarily, but he took Leigh all over the island in their spare time. They went surfing and parasailing.

They climbed Diamond Head, overlooking Honolulu. While Leigh was at work, Gregory would take her laundry over to his condo and wash, dry and fold her clothes for her, bring them back to her place so she wouldn't have to spend their time together doing it. He was very thoughtful, very devoted.

His thoughtfulness was shared through his sexuality as well. Gregory was such a sweet, lovingly gentle heart, who seemed so starved of love. He was unaccustomed to being catered to and was sincerely appreciative, reciprocating all that he was given. He was able to achieve multiple orgasms much to everyone's amazement and enjoyment. He was hiding his, a male enhancement pill, but it became obvious. What else was he hiding?

It was time for Leigh's dog to be released from quarantine, but the dog had destroyed part of the kennel he was kept in. Leigh's budget was tight and the cost of replacing it was high. She asked if she could repair it instead and the Veterinarian agreed. She purchased the needed materials, and Gregory wanted to help out. The two repaired the kennel, and the dog was released from quarantine. Gregory seemed to enjoy the dog almost as much as Leigh. He would take the dog on walks while Leigh was at work and bring him special treats. Gregory was always very thoughtful and considerate. He was having to go back to New England. His work was coming to an end on the island, but he did not want to let go of Leigh. He asked if she would marry him. Leigh was unsure. She had only known him for a few months. She had barely gotten settled into her new life, but Gregory persisted, wanting her to be a part of his life. He told her he had been divorced and had two grown daughters that he wanted her to meet. He wanted to relocate to Texas, to be with Leigh at her home. It was too much to fathom. She couldn't put it together. He had been so good to her over the past few months but why does he want to move to Texas, to be in Leigh's home? He had a home in New England but did not disclose anything more. Leigh had never had anyone treat her so well as he had. She finally agreed to his request. He bought her a little diamond ring, carved in the local Hawaiian style. He kept pushing. He wanted her to call all of her sisters and tell them she was getting married. He wanted her to tell her co-workers about him. He wanted her to give notice and move back to Texas, so after only 7 months in Hawaii, she did as her fiancée had wanted. As the time drew close for their departure, Gregory disclosed that his two daughters had devised a plan for his former wife to fly into Honolulu to meet up with him. As it turned out, he finally told Leigh the truth, that he was actually still married, and now his wife was coming and would be staying with him for a week before he returns to New England. Leigh had been lied to, ruined all of her career plans. She was totally manipulated by this man. She couldn't breathe. The wife came, and Gregory was attentive to her as Leigh watched from a distance. She had already set everything in motion and was worn out, sick from what he had done. She was ready to go back home and pick-up the pieces, starting all over again. She had sought sanctuary, but Gregory had poisoned her Honolulu.

Leigh went back home, and Gregory wanted to continue his plans to move to Texas. He came to visit, but Leigh could not believe him. Trust wasn't possible. He wanted to move from his wife's house, that she had grown up in, that his wife's parents lived in with them, into Leigh's. Gregory was deceiving his wife of over 30 years of marriage. How could Leigh expect him to treat her any better? What was his nature? How had he contrived this whole situation? He would harp on Leigh until she would oblige his wishes, even agreeing to marry him. It was time to send the Yankee back home to his wife.

Gregory did not want to give up. He continued to try to convince Leigh to take him up on his offer of marriage. He promised he would divorce his wife. He even claimed he was divorcing her and that they had attorneys but she could not be swayed. He would say anything to get what he wanted but had no care as to how it affected Leigh. She needed to somehow create a way to keep him from continuing to try to pressure her, to force his will upon her.

Chapter 7. De-bassed Andy

Back at the lake house, Leigh decided to go out one evening to avoid Gregory's contact, to try to stop dwelling on what had happened. It was a very rural town of less than 4000 with a small downtown district of old, turn of the century buildings. She found a music venue and decided to check it out. It was someone local who wasn't going to be performing for another hour. She paid a bearded, long silver-haired man at the door to attend. He told her that he didn't have tickets, but he would remember her when she came back for the show. He told her that she was welcome to bring in her own alcohol if she wanted.

Leigh drove out to the liquor store and bought a six-pack for the evening. Returning back to the little downtown, she went a few doors down to have a bite to eat at a restaurant. The man who served her a drink said he was Rick, the owner. Leigh mentioned she had some time to kill, waiting for the live music to start a few doors down. The man claimed he was a musician who had played drums for the Jeff Miller Band. He was too friendly, and it seemed odd. It was like Leigh had stumbled into some strange alternative planet where everyone knew everyone's business, and she was the visiting alien from the outskirts of Dallas. Rick ran the restaurant with his wife and two children. Get away, run. Leigh has to become more aware of the married factor. It was time for the show.

Leigh went back to the venue and sat against the wall near the door so she would be able to grab a beer out of the car as needed or vacate altogether if the show wasn't any good. She was looking around at the herd of mostly women as they started to stream in. One of them approached her. She was a scraggly-looking hippy sort in a long skirt. She said very rudely "You have to pay to attend." Leigh responded that she had paid and the guy at the door could vouch for her. The woman turned to see and he gestured to her that it was okay. She had an instant dislike of Leigh, a problem she seemed to generate so often from females. The lights dimmed, and it was some man whining into a microphone strumming a guitar. The crowd was even worse, all women wearing sparkly studded crosses and gaudy western attire. Leigh was not local. She did not have rhinestones on her pants nor flashy belt buckles and a glittery huge purse. She didn't have her hair dyed blonde, teased and coifed, with acrylic nails and bright polish. She was dressed in black and surrounded by fake. The music was terrible, but she had little else to do.

Leigh sat against the wall near the back observing the surroundings. At the back, by the door, the woman who had barred Leigh's entrance was fawning over a new arrival. He was a cute man, about a dozen years older than Leigh, with his white hair dyed blonde, but men seemed to be scarce. The woman was being very disruptive, disrespectful to the performer, but did not care in her gloating and flirting with this man. It was intermission, and Leigh was in need of another beer. She had serious doubts about staying for the rest of the performance.

Leigh hit the door. She was halfway across the street when she heard someone yelling, "Wait, Wait! You're the only nonpear-shaped woman in Winnsboro!" Now in the center of Main Street, Leigh turn to see that cute guy coming towards her and responded.

 "Uh, okay: You want a beer?"

"Well, yeah!" He hops into the passenger seat and introduces himself as Andy, talking about himself, as a professional bass player and who he had toured with professionally. Leigh introduced herself. Upon hearing her name, he choked.

 "That's my ex-wife's name." The two went back inside but decided to leave. He asked Leigh to follow him. He was driving an old little Toyota pick-up with mildew covering what was left of the paint. Following him out of town, deep into a rural area, over the county line, Leigh was becoming apprehensive, not knowing this man.

They pulled down an old one lane bumpy road. It was pitch dark. He stopped in front of an old aluminum gate, unlocking it, waving for her to follow. It was a dirt drive that led up to a small storage building that had been added onto. It had a compilation of rooms added on separated by sliding doors and a plate glass window. In the storage building, the ceiling was low just above the front door. To the left, there was a homemade staircase leading to a little-floored storage area where he had a mattress on the floor. He explained that it was his loft. You couldn't stand up and could hardly sit up in the bed. He had minimal furniture, not having any room. His coffee table consisted of a large slice of a lacquered tree trunk laid on top of a few crates, just like someone else she had known as a teenager. He had the front portion of the shed bumped out to accommodate a large race track that took up a third of his living area on a table for it, so you could stand up and race cars. He kept stuff underneath the racetrack table, openly visible. You had to turn sideways to not clip the table going into the bathroom. Behind the door of the bathroom was a half-sized hot water heater with a shelf over it and a clothes rod across the top, which served as his only closet, beside a small fiberglass shower with a loose plate covering the PVC pipe coming up as the drain. On the shower floor were bottles of expensive shampoo and conditioners. The tiny bathroom had a press-on vinyl tile flooring. There was a little drop-in style fiberglass sink with a built-in cabinet underneath that served as his dirty clothes hamper. The mirror was a medicine cabinet filled all kinds of outdated sample sizes, his whole life was in miniature. Next to the medicine cabinet was a framed serenity poem that they teach at Alcoholic Anonymous meetings. The tiny counter was littered with men's toiletries. He had a little plastic sliding cabinet over the toilet filled with stuff. While you sat on the toilet, there was a handwritten worn-out message tacked on the cheap paneling at eye level that read, "Put your toilet paper and POO paper in the trash!", next to the toilet.

The kitchen consisted of a small, double stainless sink on the reverse wall from the bathroom with a drain board for washing dishes by hand and an apartment sized refrigerator that hardly kept beer at a drinkable temperature. Through a doorway on the other side of the refrigerator, in the next built-on room, was a half-sized little range with only 2 out of the 4 burners working, and a non-operational oven used to store pans. He had a butcher block table with a little wooded single shelf across the back of it stacked full. There were two mismatched little glasses and his bottle of Whiskey. The room was used for setting up musical instruments to practice. There was a drum kit in the middle of the floor, a half a dozen guitars and bass guitars on a long rack. There was a wood stove in the far corner next to a sliding glass door that led to a little grassy knoll. There were sliding glass doors on the other two walls, one leading to a padded room with a window that had cubical partitions, musical cords, plastic milk crates filled with equipment, microphones and some guitars. There was a 3-inch thick foam piece covered with a queen sized fitted sheet leaning against the wall that served as a "mattress" for guests that he would pull out into the other room, after moving the drum kit out of the way. The last room had a raised floor that dropped down from a platform on either side and soundboard in the middle with a full-length couch at the far wall with a built-in a/c and heater unit above that made a lot of noise, running or not. There was a metal door out to the backyard hidden by drapery and a window looking out the front. He lived very differently.

They shared a few shots of his cheap whiskey and retired to his little loft. It was very cramped. Andy dozed off to sleep from the alcohol. Leigh layered quietly in his strange bed. She waited for the alcohol wore off before she collected herself, trying to sneak out. He awoke, not wanting her to leave and pleaded with her to stay the night. She reluctantly stayed, and, in the morning, he was amorous. He was cute and very aware of his attributes. He liked to be the star, being very proud and playful. He was an entertainer who had entertained a lot of women. He would take what he wanted sexually without any hesitation. He was the kind of man who took whatever he could from a woman. He was very selfish. He was his only concern. Women were to serve him.

As poor as he was he still had a woman come in and clean his house for him. Leigh was always very gracious and never critical of his way of life. Leigh was open-minded, trying not to be judgmental. She started to include Andy into her plans. He was not as accepting of her, however, and criticized Leigh constantly for what he perceived as needed changes. Her lake house wasn't good enough for him. He even would complain about her having a pool table in her dining room. Leigh thought, at least she has a dining room. She did make some modifications to make him comfortable in her home, and they stayed at her lake house as much as they were able to.

They started to see each other every day. He took her fishing in a boat that looked like a floating bathtub equipped with a smoking outboard motor that started on occasion. She had to sit on a cooler while she fished out of the back of the boat. She noticed quickly that he had an unresolved emotional issue that she tried to not to trigger. Silly things would set him off into a raging, screaming fit. He lived next door to his father, Joe. The two men loved each other as much as they hated one another and were jealous of each other in everything either did. Andy's little shack was on 8 acres. It was originally part of his father's property. His father had 50 acres and had started the plant farm many years ago. Joe had given half to Andy in a life estate and started Andy in the family business. Andy was living fast and hard with his love of Hydrocodone; his father may have expected to outlive his son. Andy took the property his father gave him and sold off the back 17 acres of it to a childhood friend and her husband, Jan and Fred. With the money from the sale of the acreage, he had the studio built onto his storage shed. His new neighbors actually improved their part of the property, building a nice brick home and stock pond on the back portion of Andy's life estate acreage.

Andy summarized his relationship with his ex-wife by saying that she could not keep her panties on while he was off working, earning a living as a musician. He married her because of a pregnancy, and they had a daughter together, Shelly. Andy never saw his daughter, who had been in and out of prison for armed robbery. She was covered with piercings and tattoos and only contacted him when she needed money.

Originally, Andy and Joe ran the plant farm together, but between their fighting, lying to each other, and their horrible tempers, they split. Leigh just let Andy talk when he wanted, not questioning or interrogating him. Andy's daughter was grown, the same age as Leigh's daughter, Jane.

Andy had quite a bit of women in his past that seemed to haunt him. He thought God was gonna send down a spaceship and save him because he was so worthy. Being a musician, the two had a connection as Artists, both being unconventional. According to Andy, Leigh "Got him", but he did not even try to understand her. Leigh expected Andy used drugs, but she didn't care what he did. She just didn't want to be a part of it. He was growing poppies and would try to harvest poppy residue from them as smoking opium.

He had been growing it for years in big pots, because no one knew how to get opium locally. He even asked Leigh if she could get him some through her clients in Real Estate. He was unbelievable.

One of the best things about their relationship was being able to get to see Andy play music, to see him perform. Leigh thoroughly enjoyed watching him and a group of guys he put together to practice. Leigh would cook and clean up after feeding the band at every practice. She tried to be as supportive as she could and not get in the way. None of them wanted a Yoko Ono thing. They were playing classic rock songs and started to try to find an audience in a town of fewer than 4000 people. It was a bright light kept in a closet. Leigh would assist like a roady, helping set up and break down what Andy allowed her to, usually the heavy stuff. Andy had a past lusting after one of the other musician's girlfriends and would frequently comment on how gorgeous she was before she had gained so much weight.

He would say that, "The light would dim when she came in a room." He always talked about how fat women were in East Texas as "Another East Texas Honey."

Leigh had a guitar she had bought for Gregory and wanted to sell it, needing money. Andy offered to sell it for her. He ended up selling it for her but did not disclose that he made $50 off of the sale of it. When she asked him about it, he wouldn't tell her. Andy was always dishonest and opportunistic. He would only do something for someone if it served his needs. He saw Leigh driving a nice car and living in a nice home and wanted to take whatever he could from her.

He told her he attended Berkshire School of Music out of Boston. She told him about her education. She asked if he graduated. He avoided discussing it and would change the subject. She looked into it and asked him what year he attended and again he would not answer. She mentioned that she was an alum at two universities, was he an alum at Berkshire? No, he wasn't. He finally gave her this story about when he lived in Boston, he had sat in on a few classes. He was never even enrolled as a student, but he would tell women that he attended school there. He faked more nonsense than anyone she had ever met. He was a curiosity to her. She understood showmanship for stage performers, but his was used for his seduction of women, the basis for him wanting to be a musician, to begin with. He was a very talented bass player but did not have the tenacity and temperament to maintain composure under pressure. He had burned many bridges having his tantrum episodes, and a few of his friends had warned Leigh. He was emotionally unstable and had a Codeine addiction that was fed by his local general practitioner who prescribed him Hydrocodone for his "anxiety", a new use or an excuse.

Now Leigh liked to relax when she went fishing. It was something she had never taken seriously, but Andy did and talked about fishing, what lures, what part of what lake, what size fish constantly. Everyone who he knew talked about fishing. Andy was going to show Leigh how it was done. He gave her the easiest rod and reel to use, not wanting her to ruin any of his good rods and reels, never mind that he had dozens of them, having been a fishing guide, but she didn't care. He would have his fits over the motor not starting or something not working correctly, so she did not want to instigate any issues. He always seemed to find them without help. At one point he asked if she wanted to learn how to drive the boat or run the trolling motor. She politely declined, knowing he would end up in the water either accidentally or on purpose. She didn't like being screamed at and would do what she could to avoid a scene. It was bad enough when she would cast, and he would be so disparaging to her. She would become tense, and the next cast, she would get caught up in a tree or on a log. He would sigh and build up to a full-on hissy fit. He liked to fish at Lake Fork, where all the real fishermen go. Leigh would have just assumed to fish on her little private lake. It was very quiet and, in her backyard, easy.

He kept telling her that, "There aren't any big Bass in that lake!", referring to the little lake. Andy hated her lake house, her little lake. He wanted a bigger lake and a woman with a bigger income. It was a cold, February day and he wanted to Bass fish. It was a nasty, freezing, wet day, even drizzling. He decided that they would fish on her little lake that day, being able to do it quickly and get back off quickly if need be. He had her fishing with a spinnerbait, and he was using a top water bait. Leigh caught a tree, a log, and no bites as they slowly drifted along the bank in the boat. He had one Bass online, but it got off before he could get it to the boat. That was all that happened in over an hour of their outing. He complained incessantly and the more he yelled, the more uncomfortable Leigh became. He was ready to go in and was carrying on about how he knew there wasn't anything worth catching in this little lake. He pointed to the side where he said she should throw next so she did. They were in front of her neighbors' dock. He kept fussing about coming out on such a cold, wet day, but sometimes that's when you catch a big one. She was quiet because she had a bite. He turns and starts scoffing, "What, you hung up again?"

She starts to reel her bite; she starts to fight as his jaw drops, "Why didn't you tell me you had a fish?" He grabs the net, and they worked the fish around the side, he nets her fish and her neighbor came running out seeing what had happened and helping Andy weigh the Bass and measure her, taking care to give her more water. She was a beautiful fish, bright green and black with stark white and huge eyes with an even bigger mouth. Her neighbor took a picture of Leigh holding her up. She was heavy, weighing 11 pounds, 10 ounces. Andy remarks about how he's never caught a fish that big before, and Leigh should be happy about it. She petted her and they let her go. She called her Magda and hoped she's do well in that little lake.

Their first Valentine's Day together was a ploy. Leigh had kept her expectation to a minimum and was low key about it. Andy had decided to give her a little box. She hesitantly opened it. It was diamond earrings. She really was shocked and very appreciative and told him so. She even bragged to her daughters about what he had given her. She wore them all of the time. Andy started to complain about her wearing them, that they scratched him, so she would take them off at bedtime and put them on the bedside table. One morning, they had disappeared completely, never to be found again. It was very strange.

After about 6 months of being back from Hawaii, Leigh had to figure out how to resolve her financial difficulties. She could not sell Real Estate in Dallas-Fort Worth from 130 miles away, and she was not established in the East Texas market. It had taken her over 2 years to build up her business that she had left behind to go to Hawaii in the first place and East Texas market was different, much slower, the nation's economy was in a tailspin.

She was amazed at how the rural people were in East Texas. She was unaccustomed to a level of dishonesty. The attitude is to totally try to take if from the other guy, especially if they are a "Pilgrim" from Dallas and don't live in East Texas full time or aren't from there originally. Stay inbred and stupid with loaded guns!

Marie was not into the whole Andy thing in her mother's life and understandably. He really treated Leigh poorly. She cared too much for him, putting up with it. It was her own fault. He wouldn't share in the birth of her granddaughter. It was too inconvenient for Andy, so she went alone. She joined Marie, and her son-in-law, Rick for the birth of Eleanor.

Andy could not resist the spotlight. Andy and Leigh had been invited to a show that his friend was performing at in downtown Dallas. Many of his old musician buddies were there. Andy never took Leigh out unless he was performing somewhere local, and then Leigh had to work, helping out carrying equipment. This was probably the best night out they had. He had so much fun, and she enjoyed taking pictures of them having fun, playing. The whole place was having a good time. They ended up spending the night at his musician friends' house. His last live-in girlfriend did not like Leigh at all, the usual response she got from other women, especially when they don't know her at all. Leigh tried not to hiss at her and had to get up and go to a mortgage counseling center in downtown the next morning. Leigh got up before anyone was awake and showered. When she was drying off, one of Andy's' buddies opened the door, staring at her from the doorway. She glared at him and gestured for him to shut the door. He just grinned; dirty old man!

Leigh continued to look for work. She even took a job the local discount department store to try to take care of her bills. As a result, she ended up getting a Real Estate related job back in Hawaii. She was able to also transfer her hourly job with discount department store, to work overnight on Kauai. She was working 32 hours a week with the discount department store and 40 hours a week with the County of Kauai. She wore herself out. She became incoherent, living in a house, renting a room with roommates that ate all of her food and did not make allowances for a daytime sleeper. She was having trouble with her renters in her Dallas home. Her dog was at Jane's house in Texas. She could not get a footing where she was at and with each passing day, her health was declining. She did not need much of a push to come back to Texas from the last boyfriend, Andy, with all of his promises to get married, move in and help with her mortgage if she would just come back home.

On her return flight to Texas, Leigh was so exhausted, she began to feel very sick. Being in the window seat, she had to wake the two seated next to her on the long flight. She passed out in the aisle, trying to get to the restroom. She woke up, thinking how much better she felt. Suddenly she realized she had passed out and was laying in the middle of the isle on the airplane. Her first thought was, "Oh no, where am I!" She was so embarrassed. They ended up deplaning her first with paramedics waiting. They tested her vital signs and took blood to make sure she wasn't on any drugs. They told her that had an irregular heartbeat, a heart arrhythmia, and that she should see a doctor as soon as she got home. The airline bumped her on an earlier connecting flight and got her home as quickly as they could.

She should have paid attention to her initial insight, feelings and continued on her path, but she second-guessed herself and returned to Andy after he begged, pleaded and promised to be her husband and partner. Leigh walked away from any security, the government job that she had set up everything around, a second time for the sake of a man, for promises that he made to her. Andy had agreed to pick her up at the airport. She had kept him updated with her changing flight schedule, but he was over 30 minutes late picking her up, after her ordeal. He seemed a little lackluster in his first sight of her. He had been emailing her about how much he missed her and how he wanted her to be his wife but even in the phone calls and emails, something seemed to be missing. He and one of his buddies, Raymond, had decided that they were going to build a surprise for Leigh's return. Andy had this waiting for her at his house. It was a spanking bench.

Now they had not been having any masochistic behavior in their relationship. What was this about? He had the studio littered with sex toys that he bought and even some that he made himself. He was going to teach her a lesson, or so he thought. Leigh really wanted to leave right then and there, knowing she had made a serious mistake coming back for him.

Andy did not want to let go of their relationship. Leigh felt like there were too many issues between them to expect it to last. He would tell his friends that "God put us together for a reason, she's blind and I'm deaf." but he was not treating her like a partner. When she would help him with the plant farm, he would put all of the hardest work in her lap. She would have to carry the bags. She would do the lifting. He would walk off and leave her with all of it. It was never quid pro quo, it was never fair and even. He thought of himself as an important musician, a star who shouldn't have to do the hard work if he could get someone else to do it for him. He wanted someone with money, but they had to be slim, attractive, and give him control. He was not a manly man. He was cowardly and would put the blame on a woman if he could. He would talk about his friend Raymond and his "bitch of a wife who spends all of his money..." despite the fact they have three kids and she works too. In his mind, it was always the woman's fault for anything that was wrong. He was really masochistic and it started to show in everything he did. When he would start to lose his temper and start screaming, Leigh would grab her arm like something was hurting, pecking at it and say, "Ow, oww!" He stopped fussing and looked at Leigh holding her arm and ask, "What, what's wrong?" She would say "I'm being henpecked!" and laugh at him. She would try to use humor as a way to defuse his temper. If he started to build up tension, getting into a rage, she would tell him "You're acting just like a woman!" to get him to stop.

Leigh played along, imitating his behavior as a way to get through. He truly hated women, having been abandoned by his own mother twice. He blamed his father for her leaving. He not only hated Leigh but wanted her to fail and did all he could to bring her down.

He kept trying to get Leigh to take the sex toys and spanking bench he made to her house. She didn't want it in her house. She had grandchildren who visited and did not want something like that under her roof. He brought it over anyway, putting it in Leigh's driveway. She took it and doused it with gasoline and had a little bonfire. The next time he came over, Leigh pointed to the charred remains of his bench and destroyed the toys as well. Oddly enough, he had run over the remains of his bench and had gotten a couple of flat tires as a result. It was too funny, but the real joke was on her. She could not find work and got further and further behind trying to hang on to her two houses with no help from him. He denied what he had promised her and watched her struggle as she began failing, falling further and further behind on her mortgages and debt.

Andy always had cheap beer. He would buy an 18 pack and have a roady on the way back from the liquor store. He kept a bottle of cheap whiskey for the evening. He usually reserved his hard liquor for the weekend, but not always. It mainly depended upon what he had to try to accomplish for that day. Andy stressed over everything and would need a beer to calm down. If it was afternoon and he was in the truck, he had an open container and would throw the can out the window when he was finished, saying that it gave the poor something to make money with, picking up his discarded cans. He would stress If someone followed him too closely driving. On the way back from the liquor store, a big truck was tailgating him, driving very aggressively. Andy wasn't in the mood and wanted to fight. He started getting redder and madder the harder the truck pursued. Andy yelled at Leigh to, "Get the hammer out from behind the seat. We're going to pull over and beat the shit out of this hillbilly!" Leigh paused and tried to pull him back from the edge of crazy. "Do you think that's going to make things better. What if he has a gun?" That quelled his anger. Puffs of his verbal smoke followed, "I'll remember you, you asshole!"

Andy was allergic to red wasp, so Leigh would make a point to try to kill them anywhere around his house and in the greenhouses. He had one large greenhouse and a half-sized one that Fred had used but abandoned. Both had metal bows and clear plastic coverings with a large fan on either end. The large house had a swamp cooler. He had PVC piping with a water spigot that pumped from a well that Andy shared with his father's property. There was electricity and woven plastic matting for the floor. The red wasp seemed to converge on his place. He told Leigh he kept an epi pen if he got stung. As much as she killed the wasps, she would try to set the dragonflies, butterflies, and moths free from his greenhouses. They would become trapped inside and die. He would sweep up piles of the little-winged creatures, being such a waste. He kept several cans of wasp spray on hand and had a fly swatter by a little rocking chair he sat in on his porch. He had things piled around his porch, his rusting tools were left on the side of his shed like home. He had dishes underneath his front porch deck and a barrage of junk in between his outdoor propane burner for frying fish, smoker and grill. There was a homemade porch swing in disrepair. There was usually an empty dirtbag from the greenhouse filled with beer cans and a few empty bottles of cooking oil strewn about.

Leigh tried to approach their relationship with humor. With him being so much older than she was, she would tease him. They would be driving through Longview, by a senior citizen center, and she would tell him she could go in there and have her pick of the litter for her next boyfriend and get one with a good retirement that wore depends for easy cleanup. Andy and Leigh would go to the thrift store, and they would just assume he knew it was senior discount day being Wednesday and give him his discount. He would glare at her, snickering about him not even being carded.

On one of their trips to the local discount department store, they came across an older woman with bleached hair teased up, dressed in pink sparkles and stilettos, pushing a little girl through the Barbie aisle. Andy and Leigh had to turn away at the sight. Leigh started a story about Barbie and Ken and how she got the beach house and Corvette in the divorce, but all Ken got was away.

Andy's father, Joe had been going to dances with the other seniors for years. They would all meet up in Hawkins or at other designated dance halls and have an evening of social interaction and some exercise to some awful country music being performed by some local wanna-be county band. Joe liked the ladies, and at his age, now 78, they liked a man with cancer as a hope for some life insurance benefits or property if they could woo him. He liked the attention, and so the game was on. The women would be relentless. One in particular, Wanda, started coming to his house. She was not willing to be intimate with him unless he was going to marry her. She had not figured out that Joe wasn't able to be intimate with his prostate cancer, but he got what he could out of their tryst. She would come over and make him cherry cake from a box and cook all sorts of toxic foods that Andy and Leigh would cringe at. She would follow him around in his greenhouses and try to get into his business affairs. She was a little bigger than he was, and Andy and Leigh referred to her as the horse-faced woman that needed a saddle. Even Joe grew tired of her intrusion and chased her off.

Joe's property consisted of about 26 heavily forested acres. One of his little girlfriends had convinced him to have all of the wood harvested, essentially raping trees from the acreage. It looks like the remains of a war zone stripped bare. They all knew each other and tried to get into each other's pocket. Joe did not have a wife, but he had property. This ruined the beauty of the acreage and scarred it permanently. Andy was livid, because he was the sole heir.

Andy's father had prostate cancer for years. Being a veteran, he would go to the Veterans' Hospital for treatment, but

Leigh took him for the last time early that Spring, and they basically had stopped providing him any care. He came home without having any additional treatment and was having problems just trying to have regular bowel movements. It turned toxic for him, and he had to be admitted into the local hospital in Quitman. They could not do anything for him except keep him sedated. They even put him on a morphine drip, so he could hit a button if he was in too much pain, to self-administer another dose. Joe had many girlfriends but did not want any of them close. He suffered from the side effects from his prostate cancer. Several of his little dance hall girlfriends wanted to visit Joe, but Andy chased them off. He did not want his father to have any visitors. He wanted him to be all alone. Andy would not stay with his father either and left him, knowing it was the end of his path. Joe died alone in a dark room. Andy received a phone call from the hospital later that evening. He was lying in his bed. No one had tended to him. His mouth was agape and he was cold. His medicine had been raided and Leigh tried to get some answers from one of the Charge Nurses on duty. The one that showed up was a young man and his eyes were dilated, he was high on something. He realized Leigh knew and hid from her as she started to question him about Joe's missing prescription medicine. Joe's fight was over with cancer and between the two men, father and son. Andy was left his father's property, $17,000 from the sale of the timber and another little life insurance policy that he had to collect from an insurance man in Gilmer.

Leigh watched Andy delay and not put forth the effort to take care of Joe after his death. It was put on her to figure out how to take care of Joe's body, to find out what to do, to have his death certificates made, to have his body picked up by the funeral home, to have his body cremated, how much it was going to cost, to figure out how to do this. She was sick over it. He could not do for his own father. He did not want to have a funeral for his own father, and some of Joe's dancehall friends put together a service at a local little church for him. Andy was more concerned with where his own Hydrocodone was. Leigh stayed with Andy and met with his family that flew in to console him, but he was unbelievable to her. He could not even spread his father's ashes. He completely withdrew, and it made Leigh angry that he could be so selfish about his father's passing and not do what had to be done.

Andy went off the deep end as Leigh struggled not to lose her house to foreclosure. She was having to go to Dallas to clean up her home after the last tenants, hoping to move back in. Andy showed up, barging into her home expecting to see her with another man, accusing her of having an affair, that her previous married boyfriend was there helping her. Leigh was busy cleaning up and painting. She just shook her head and handed him a paintbrush, sending him upstairs. He could not say anything nice and kept complaining about how he hated her house, how awful it was, how it was a piece of trash. She thought after she had gone out of her way not to criticize him, and now he could not show her any respect, having no regard for her feelings, expecting the worst of her only to find that he was completely wrong again. Just go to hell, Andy! While they are apart, Andy begins burning through his dad's money, selling and buying vehicles, selling one truck and buying another just like it while Leigh was facing foreclosure, fighting with the wolves.

Leigh had tried to keep her job working at local discount department store with an overnight schedule, but Andy was sure she was sleeping with someone from work. He never moved in as promised, and no relief came. She had to ask Gregory for financial help just to try to hang on and he obliged her. He may have lied to her but he was still willing to help when she asked. Leigh tried to find a job anywhere she could to be able to hang on, and the only thing that opened up was in Winnsboro. She managed to get a job working as a Human Resource Manager for a local manufacturing company for $11.50 an hour. It was not enough to cover both houses, and she knew it. She felt like the dye had been cast, and she was to stay at the lake house being that that was where her new job was. Andy would not stay away, and she was all alone. She cared too much and she felt like she could not say no to the crazy man no matter how she tried to talk reason to herself. He was her weakness. He was bad for her. She was hooked just like a fish.

Andy decided they needed to take a trip together. She had no business taking a trip. She had no money and was doing all she could to hang on to her lake house. He wants to check out his old stomping grounds in Austin, find his old hangouts, where he had been when he was in his late teens. Looking online, he decided on a hotel a few blocks from downtown that seemed like a neat kind of eclectic place, but he did not bother to make reservations. On the way to Austin, they had to go find a boat he wanted to buy from some boat dealer in Rockwall. At the dealer's, Andy paid the man and ogled his newer boat, a fiberglass bass boat, white with sparkly red metallic and gold trim, a bullet, a huge improvement over the old bathtub sidewinder. They would pick it up on their way back from Austin. Finally, on the outskirts of town, it was getting late Andy had to pull over and let Leigh drive, he could not handle the 5 o'clock traffic. They got to downtown and found this place he was so excited about, but the only room they had available was more than double of what they showed online. He started to get even more agitated. He left Austin to get away from the traffic. He started up, too much money, too much traffic. Leigh thought you, idiot. You are too unprepared. You have been here before and know how long it takes. That they would hit traffic going when they did, and you did not plan anything and just drove around to try to find what you could remember from 50 years ago. Watching this, she did not say a word. It wouldn't do any good anyhow, and she would have to listen to him scream and complain. She did what she could to minimize his rages. She drove to Marble Falls, and they stayed at a little bed and breakfast and had a great Thai dinner. It was the high point. Andy could not be intimate in a hotel, away from home. He had to sit up and read his operating brochures on his new boat waiting for him in Rockwall. He started obsessing over it, wanting to be with his boat, not Leigh. They drove around the outskirts, but Andy just complained about needing to get back to see his boat. The following morning, they stopped at Krause Springs and spent most of the day swimming in the spring and tromping around the grounds. They tried to go into Austin, but the traffic was too much for Andy. They started back but stopped at an underground cavern. It was very interesting, but Andy was too distracted. He wanted to go and get his boat, and that's just what they were going to do. He was at the level of a two-year-old in so many ways. They stopped and picked up the boat. Leigh was surprised he didn't sit in it while she drove back. Andy blew through the rest of his inheritance on two more trucks and started on collecting guns. He was busy giving away his father's money. The local mechanic knew he had just lost his father and had money from his death and took advantage of him as well.

Andy never understood Leigh as a Real Estate Broker with her own business. He prided himself on his chili. She was not much for chili but thought he would enjoy an opportunity to have others assess his chili effort. She entered the Board of Real Estate's annual chili cook-off, paying to be a part of the event. He fussed and fussed the entire way to the event that, "This was the stupidest thing you ever made me do!" She had to have a sports theme so they were the golf tent. You had to putt down the green and get the golf ball in the hole for a Guinness. Leigh had to quickly remind Andy that minors did not get a beer. Leigh made cookies and brought an ice chest full of Guinness. She set everything up while he got going on something other than complaining, starting to cook. He felt better after a few beers, and after he realized all the other people she knew. They stopped by the tent and visited with Andy and Leigh. Ed came too and camped out at their tent. It was nice to see all of her old business acquaintances. They all seemed to love his chili so he wanted to check out the competition. He was so excited, knowing his was by far, the best. He wanted Leigh to try everyone else's, but she really did not like chili and avoided bad chili. He was a little worried about the braggers across the lane from them showing off their trophies from years past. He became nervous as they collected samples for the judges. They collected them in a blind sampling. It was getting dark, late, and Leigh started to clean up for her long drive home. They had started awarding the best tent, the best reward for a tent, the best moneyearning tent, and finally, the best chili. Leigh was throwing away trash out back, and Ed called out to her, "Leigh! They called your company!" She went and got Andy, and they accepted the first-place trophy. He was so proud of himself. She sent him home with the trophy, and he told everyone he knew that he won a chili cook-off. He kept it on display in his little family room. He never thanked her nor apologized.

At Andy's, watching the evening news, the politics were getting heated, and Leigh couldn't stand what she is watching. Andy asked her out of the blue, "How many men have you been with?" She's not paying attention to him, fussing at the news, "All those fucking Republicans!" She paused and looked at him realizing what he had asked and burst out laughing at his inquiry. This question coming from a sexually promiscuous musician on the loose since he was a preteen, out to screw as many women as his penis could before if falls off was beyond hilarious.

Leigh could not hang on to the home in Dallas and could not re-establish her Real Estate career and business that she had worked so long and hard to build up. She was under a lot of stress financially going through the process of foreclosure and had to remove her belongings from the home. Andy would not help, he did not do manual labor. Instead one of his plant farm workers help her. She rented a truck worked all day loading the truck, returning back to East Texas.

Leigh continued to look for a better job, even trying to get her old job back with the State of Hawaii. She had to go to Honolulu for the interview desperate for work, scraping together enough to go with the help of her sister, Jeanie, staying as cheaply as she could, at a hostel, like Huston had taught her. At the interview, she was told by one of her former associates that she was qualified, but she just wasn't convinced that Leigh would stay this time and they picked someone else as a result. Andy just knew Leigh met up with Gregory and had a little dalliance.

Andy decided that his boat wasn't comfortable. He couldn't see over the front of the boat while driving and the cost of the boat was starting to show, so he sold it back to the guy he bought it from. Andy finds an aluminum boat for sale by owner as a less expensive alternative, an Express boat. It was smaller and cheaper to maintain, but he did not consider the size of his most frequent fishing guide client being over 6 ft. tall and over 250 pounds. The latest boat lilted under the weight of his portly client.

Leigh was needing to have her eyesight checked and made an appointment with a specialist, being that glaucoma ran in her family. It was her mother's doctor. After doing an exam, the doctor required Leigh to have laser surgery right away. She had narrow closure glaucoma and had too much pressure on her eyes that could cause immediate blindness. Calling Andy, she asked permission to use his credit card for the procedure, not having the money herself but needing it done according to the Doctor. Andy blew up at the request. She tried to reason with him, promising to pay him back as soon as she was able. He was unbelievable, despite that Leigh waited on him hand and foot, cooked for him, washed his clothes, had him staying at her house. Now, when she really needed his help he wanted to deny her. This changed her eyesight permanently for the worse and her night vision was declining too. She started painting more, pulling inward, not wanting to have Andy in her life. He was toxic with his required daily intake of alcohol, selfishness and ridiculous accusations that were reflecting his own behavior. He did not understand Real Estate, working with clients and any business Leigh had. He would yell at her, adding stress to an already difficult job, never being supportive, just jealous and ugly.

Andy liked to start Summer evenings with a drink lounging on Leigh's dock. He would have his whiskey and she would have her wine. He had been tipping back a few and told her about a band that had owed him for some studio time and that they had stiffed him. This band was a local band performing at a bar about 30 minutes North. He wanted to have Leigh slip in backstage and take a few of their guitars, because they owed him money and refused to pay him. Leigh went along with his idea to see where the path led. He was serious, even trying to figure out what car she should drive while committing this crime for him. So, it's settled, she was to go on this designated night and get back stage prior to the performance and slip out the back with their guitars. Leigh laughed at him and told him he really did not know her at all, and he was an idiot. He backed off, "Oh, I'm just kidding…" No, and you are a criminal who hangs things on women.

Knowing his past behavior, he would probably call the police on her during the theft. Why was she in this relationship? How could she care about such a bad person who would intentionally cause her harm? What was wrong with her, why can't she shake this thing between them?

Fishing together, Andy would locate fish on his graph and tell Leigh the depth. She would measure off however many feet and clip her line and reel it back up. Then she would try to cast the lure and let it drop to that depth in a free fall, emulating a real fish more so that up and down. She started catching crappie. Andy would always fuss at Leigh if she did not say anything. She was usually pretty quiet about it because he would turn the boat and move himself in the catbird seat, front boating her where she could not get back to the spot as well. He did this so often that she wouldn't even worry about it. "Fine, catch all the fish yourself." She would just sit back and drink all of his beer. On one of their fishing expeditions, Leigh had taken off her expensive sunglasses, putting them in the seat, not wanting to drop them in the water while she was pulling in a fish. Andy, uncharacteristically came to the back of the boat, stepping on her sunglasses in the seat with a crunch. She gave him an ugly look, but he started yelling at her that it was her fault, she left them in the seat. Well, where the hell is she gonna leave them, on the floor? "You're gonna buy me a new pair.", was her response. He screamed even more that it was her fault. He reluctantly bought her another pair after he consulted with one of his buddies, who he was getting his advice from. It wasn't her. After you have been with someone for so long, you can tell when someone else is whispering in their ear, whether it is his thinking or someone else's. He started listening to one of his newest fishing buddies. Leigh was the reason for all of Andy's problems, so just get rid of her. She should have known better, but she wanted to believe that he was better than he was, that he loved her, but he just loved how she made him feel.

The next concert Andy's band had, he made a little trophy for his band as a joke out of a "Steely Dan" dildo and had an engraved plaque mounted at the bottom for the band to be awarded at their show in Downtown Winnsboro. They had to really work to fill up the room. The band was great, but the audience was limited in such a small town in the middle of nowhere, and everyone had already seen them perform on several other occasions. It wasn't anything new to anyone locally.

Andy set up a Tyler venue, but it coincided with an outdoor concert on the square. Andy's band was booked to play for a high school reunion at a restaurant on their patio. It was a hot night, and one of the headliners for the concert on the square had visited Andy's studio a week before, inquiring about Andy's band and their next show in Tyler. This other band took Andy's playlist and were performing it at their stage simultaneously. Andy was pissed. Leigh was bored and wanted to see what the competition he had was doing. She did not have any money but was able to walk into the outdoor concert beside a group of people who had tickets. They were doing the best they could to reproduce Andy's song list and had a much larger crowd being outdoors, having other bands taking part in the show. Leigh walked around and saw what she wanted and went back to the patio, even getting stamped so she could return to the outdoor concert if she wanted. Andy saw Leigh return and came up to her in a tither, ready to fight. He grabbed her sunglasses from her and said he would keep them. "No, I'll put them in the car." He felt like they were his, just like the diamonds he gave her and took back, forgetting that he broke her other sunglasses.

He had been busy while she was gone and started accusing her of having some man pay for her concert ticket outdoors. She told him what she did, and he just knew she was lying. He started to forcibly grab for her glasses, and she pulled away. He had to go on stage now. Leigh decided she would see what he was causing a fight over. He had his eye on someone down by the stage. As his band started to play, Leigh came down to the front row and plopped next to a woman a little older than her but who was watching Andy intently. She began telling Leigh how cute Andy was and how Andy told her he went to the Berkeley School of Music out of Boston. Leigh laughed at what had gone on. He had set himself up a lay for the evening and was trying to get rid of Leigh, but unfortunately, she did not drive, riding with Andy. Leigh told the woman that he never attended Berkeley, he says he just sat in on a few classes, and they both had a laugh. On stage, Andy could not concentrate on his playing and moved a fan, attempting to be able to hear the two women better, and blew his music off of his music stand, all over the stage. Leigh chatted up the woman, and she was now into Leigh instead of Andy. She stole his groupie away. Andy had a meltdown and fought with Leigh on the floor, creating a scene. She was in tears, seeing everything he was about. She went inside and had to figure out how to get home. The bar Manager wanted to take her home, but he made his intentions clear. She had to beg another band member to take her back home. All of his band treated Leigh like she had the plague and she did, the Andy plague.

One of the guys in the band, Brent decided to rent Andy's father's house from Andy with his new wife, Amy, and their daughter. Brent was having a hard time at work and was going to be fired. It wasn't a surprise and was expected. Andy worked with them on paying him rent. Brent had always been a late arrival for practice, but now he had no excuse to be late. He showed up in a bad way, grinding his teeth and unable to practice in his condition. He was on speed, with high blood pressure and dilated eyes. He started jabbering about not being able to sleep, and that he had some sleeping pills now from his doctor. Leigh saw what was going on and walked him back to the rent house and told his wife that she really needed to help him, he was not doing well. Amy became vulgar towards Brent and disgusted by Leigh's presence. Leigh left him with her, knowing that he was not going to be the same ever again. It really felt like it was the end of their band, and the end for Brent.

July was a strange month for the band. At the last outdoor concert at the local bakery, Brent was too high to perform. He had lost his way. He couldn't seem to find contentment and would wander off, doing solo performances, trying to find his way musically. Andy had worked with the band putting together an album, and it was almost completed. Andy asked Leigh to put together something for the album cover, and she designed caricatures of each of the band members as skeletons in a boat. Andy loved it and wanted to use it. Just as everything was done and ready to put out the band's first album, Brent had an overdose and was in the hospital. He had mixing sleeping pills and speed. Brent died at 37. Andy became angry at how "stupid he was!" Andy showed more concern for an expensive guitar that Brent had left it in his vehicle. "The heat will ruin it." Andy took it back to his house. Leigh saw him take things from her and others throughout the years and did not want that to happen with Brent's guitar. Leigh told Amy that Andy had taken it. She was in such a confused state, looking at Leigh like she was a crazy woman. Andy returned it after he realized Leigh had told Amy what he had done. Leigh did not trust Andy. The guitar belonged to Amy.

Leigh was painting. She had just finished a project of 16 angels, oil paintings of statuary from cemeteries around Texas and decided to try to put them on display in front of people to see their response, knowing that the East Texas market wasn't ideal for her gothic art, but she felt like she had to get over her fear of rejection artistically. So, she made plans to participate in the local event known as the "First Monday" in Canton. She paid to have a spot and brought her tent and set up her display as intended. While she was out mixing with the locals in the dusty field, hearing the remarks good and bad, she received a call from the gallery that participated in the Fort Worth Gallery Night tour. She was invited to show some of her work during the gallery night. She packed up and left the dusty venue behind.

The gallery owner was one of Ed's old classmates from high school. It had been run by the same old family since Ed could remember, and he knew them personally. He was the lead

Leigh had for her work and she took a few pieces to show the curator, JT. He had picked three of her paintings and she was so excited. She even talked Andy into coming to the exhibit. The day of "Fort Worth Gallery Night", Leigh's father was down the street in hospice at the local hospital.

Andy came to the show. Leigh looked around for her work, but only found one hanging in a hallway next to the bathroom with JT's sister's work above it. Hers was also a face of a statuary. She was telling someone about how she just whipped it up really quick a last-minute watercolor. Nepotism was alive and hanging on the wall next to Leigh's work as an attempt to boost interest JT's sibling's. Leigh's other two pieces were lying on the floor sandwiched in between other paintings, tilted against a wall, without anything to protect the work. Leigh was not going to do this again. Leigh, Andy, and Ed toured other galleries and did not see this type of poor treatment anywhere else. Leigh bought Ed's lunch at Lucile's, and Andy complained that Leigh needed to buy his too.

Leigh's father died a few weeks later, and her sisters flew in for his memorial and funeral. Leigh had to attend by herself. Andy did not show her any consideration at all unlike what she had shown him with his father's passing.

Andy loved Joni Mitchell. He would carry on about how wonderful her music was, but Leigh was unfamiliar with her work so she bought a bunch of CD's to play while Andy was in the car as a way to try to quell his bad behavior. He would have tantrums when she was driving and talking on the phone with clients and she needed to have a distraction for the two-year-old behavior, to be able to take care of the business she had. At one point, she was driving and talking with Huston on her cell phone, and Andy just exploded because she was not paying attention to him. She wanted to pull over and let him out. She ended her call and took a breath, watching him flailing and screaming over nothing.

Leigh dropped him off to pick up his truck. He had backed into a sign resulting in some body damage. The guy at the body shop was thankful to be done with Andy. He was amazed at how much of a pest he had become about his truck being repaired and complimented Leigh on her patience in dealing with him. Unfortunately, even Joni wasn't enough to help some days.

Leigh had been feeding a feral cat, a small bob-tailed orange tabby. She could not get close to her and one morning the cat showed up on her screened porch with 2 kittens. Leigh warmed up some milk and needed to figure out how to get that cat fixed. She was going to keep having kittens if she did not do something. She kept feeding the three, and one day, the mama cat was missing again. She had 3 more kittens. Now there were six, and the first batch would soon be old enough to have kittens themselves. Leigh found a local charity that helped with the feral cat population, "Pets Fur People", and they subsidized having them fixed. Leigh set it up with the local veterinarian clinic to bring all of the cats in to be fixed. Now all she had to do was catch them and bring them to the Vet. She did not have a trap but she had two cat carriers. She decided that she would feed them her laundry room a few times a few days in advance, getting them used to going in there and then on the day of their appointments, she would trap them in the laundry room from the outside door and catch them, putting them into the cat carriers and then off to the vet. Andy did not want to help but he wanted to watch. He claimed with his thinning skin, he would bleed too easily. Leigh was able to get the cats to eat as planned but, on the day, she was to trap them, not all of them showed up for breakfast. Two were missing. She had shut 4 of the cats in the laundry room, and you could hear the pandemonium. Howls, cries of the trapped animals bellowed from the laundry room. Andy watched as Leigh prepared to go in there, but first she had to finish her coffee. Leigh took a deep breath and put on her leather coat and gloves. She entered from the kitchen, Andy squeezed in behind her. The cats were climbing the walls in a swirl of cats in the laundry room. She grabbed the closest one on the wall by the scruff. It fought fiercely as a little tiger, as she tossed it into a carrier, shutting the door behind it. She grabbed for another as Andy tried to help, opening a carrier door and another one was in, but Andy was skittish of the flying claws and fur, not shutting the door all of the way, one escapes. Leigh worked on catching another, but it bites her through her glove. She is spewing blood as she grabbed it and tossed it in the second carrier. She looked at her cuts, trying to stay focused and grabbed another cat and getting it into the second carrier too. Leigh catches the last one and puts it in the first cage again, safely locked inside. The cats are crying a howling, protesting their capture as the hiss and claw from inside the containers. Leigh and Andy loaded the two carriers into the back of Leigh's vehicle lined with towels. At the vet's office, Leigh takes them inside. She sees that she is not the only one with feral cats. Everyone else had traps. Leigh just had carriers. Andy was speechless. He mentioned that he knew who he would take to a knife fight if he had to, referring to Leigh plowing through what had to be done. The vet tech took the cats out by dumping them into a pillowcase. Then they could hold each cat down and give them a shot without being bit or clawed. Leigh mentioned she had to catch two more and would be back. Leigh caught another cat later that evening. The last cat, the long-haired and only male, she caught the next day. Leigh had been bitten a few times and was feeling the effects of what seemed like hydrophobia. Leigh felt like she would never be able to clear her thoughts again. Leigh began to have the most vivid and frightening dreams she had ever had her life. About a week later, it had worsened and she went and got a tetanus shot. Andy's doctor would not see Leigh. He claimed he would not take any new patients, but he prescribed Andy some medicine that would help her. It took a few weeks for her to feel like she wasn't losing her mind and months before she felt like herself. It was indescribable and overwhelming.

Late one evening, Andy and Leigh had been drinking. It had gotten to the point that if she did not have any intimacy with Andy in the morning, she would not get another opportunity. Being that Andy was so much older and had high blood pressure, she never initiated things, but the alcohol had become his mistress. He had no interest in her. She was upset, and he was sick of her climbing into the wine bottle. She dove in early that night. What was the point? She can't stand this separate arm's length. She had her home and he had his. What was his being his and what was hers' was his to use? She thought "Fine, let go and let me get on with my life.

You can't have it both ways." Andy had been building into a hateful state the entire day. Leigh began avoiding him, not wanting to set him off into a tantrum. It didn't matter. To add to the tension, Leigh could not just go home, her daughter was visiting, needing some time away from her husband. She didn't want to interfere with her daughter's situation either.

Leigh and her daughter were very close. Leigh had left her vehicle at her house, so Andy was in control of her coming and going back home. Andy was jealous of Leigh's daughter, underscoring the bad relationship he had with his own. He was upset with nothing and everything and aimed his anger at Leigh. Leigh was on his porch, staying outside, away from Andy. He finds her sitting on the porch swing and grabs the wine bottle, smashing it into pieces, frightening Leigh. Leigh ran inside to avoid Andy's rage. He corners her next to the refrigerator and screams at her. She had been drinking wine out of an old cup her mother had given her when she graduated from the university. It was very sentimental to her with a little tiger on it. Andy grabbed the cup out of her hands and smashed it into tiny pieces. Both had been drinking most of the afternoon. He had been getting angrier and angrier building into a full-blown emotional explosion. Both were drunk. Leigh was fearful and called the police. Once he realized what she had done, he calmed down, so she told them on her call, never mind. Leigh tried to leave, not having her car she had to walk. She could not find her shoes. He had taken them. Not being able to see in the dark, she put on a pair of his. She only lived 6 miles away and she was not going to let him hurt her. She left but he called the cops on her. He knew some of the local cops through one of his buddies, whose son-in-law was a police officer. Leigh got about a half mile down the street and the squad car pulls up and he arrests her. "What, I'm just walking home!" "You're drunk, and you have to come with me!" "Andy called didn't he!" "Yep." "That Ass." Leigh was taken to jail trying to walk home after Andy started throwing things at her. In Jail, Leigh was stripped while being videoed. She was pissed and drunk. Leigh told one of the fattest police officers that he was a disgusting failure, that he could not catch a criminal and should be ashamed that our tax dollars are being wasted on his gluttony. They kept her there overnight. Leigh was waiting to go before the judge and Andy showed up about 8:00 the following morning. He was acting like it was her fault, and that she was going to have to pay him back for bailing her out. She told him "not to bother, I'll see the Judge". She told him she knew he called the police to pick her up. He denied it, and she told him again and that the cop told her that he did. He shut up. He was caught lying to her and causing her intentional harm after how he treated her. "Go to hell!"

Again, the split. Leigh always got a lot done not having to take care of Andy and finished her Water Project paintings. Andy shows up on her screened porch just like the feral cats she fed. Both were lonely, missing what had become too familiar with carrying things forward in silence. He brought her broken little tiger cup back to her. He had glued the tiny pieces back together as a peace offering. He wanted to go out to Cypress Springs and see Brian, a successful, self-made Cajun man who had a custom home on Lake Cypress Springs that had enjoyed Andy's musical talent who was also an avid fisherman. He had been dating a former school teacher,

Tonya, who believed in too much of the Cajun voodoo and was terrified of cats. While the pair were out fishing under a highway bridge, there was a tiny little kitten clinging onto a pillion under the bridge. Someone had thrown the poor creature off the bridge, into the lake, and it was hanging on trying not to drown. Brian fished it out with his net, and now the tiny kitten was circling his lake house trying to find a new mother. Tonya wouldn't have it, but Andy would. It was a tiny little orange tabby that couldn't have been more than 2 or 3 weeks old. He took it in, but his other cat, Mini, was not happy about this little intrusion. The little kitten was so sweet and so loving. He continued to try to make friends with Mini, but she wouldn't have it. Andy and Leigh named the kitten Bridgett, having been thrown off a bridge, but she turned out to be a Bud.

After fishing with Andy for several years, Leigh never pushed him, always letting the breeze blow their relationship where it may. Easter rolled around, and Andy wanted to go fishing on Lake Fork Easter Sunday. He had never gotten Easter Baskets as a child, so Leigh would usually put a basket together for him. He would just buy her a bottle of wine. Leigh put together a basket of chocolates and included a shiny cape, mask and bunny ears for Andy to become "Super Bunny", posing for pictures in his little camper. After enough whiskey, Andy had no boundaries of behavior. He must have had some other fish he wanted to catch. Leigh was disgusted by his lack of loyalty. He had no respect for her, nor any other women. He was out to get whatever he could from any woman he could. One of the buddies referred to Andy's little camper as the "Stabbin Cabin", and Leigh was so uncomfortable there. Everyone could hear everything that went on and they all either played switch your partner or didn't have any sex at all. Leigh didn't want any part of the nonsense. One of his neighbors was a local police officer, out there with his wife and children on weekends. They would have a bonfire and toast marshmallows and drink on into the evening. Weeks after Andy and Leigh had another split, this police friend of his shows up at her lake house. He had been drinking and Leigh asked him what was up if Andy sent him by. "No, I just wanted to come and see you." Leigh asked him if his wife was doing okay and sent him on down the road.

Andy decided to sell his father's house with the 25 acres across the creek from his studio, so Leigh put Andy's father's property up for sale and wrote up a listing agreement, cutting her commission for him. She started advertising it in MLS and put a sign-out. Word had gotten around about the property, and she helped a buyer work a deal where Andy would seller finance for a few years with interest and receive a monthly mortgage payment from the buyers. This enabled a family, new to the area, to live in a home instead of the recreation vehicle they had been living in with 5 children. Leigh wrote the contract and walked everyone through the process, set up the surveyor and handled the issues Andy had about the property line and got everyone to the closing table, signed and executed. But this wasn't enough for Andy. Andy was mad at Leigh about her commission and constantly complained about what Leigh had earned. She ended up giving him $500. just to shut him up. He did not see how important what she did was nor that she had any ability or value.

At his studio, Andy's cat Mini would not accept Bud. She would keep as much distance between the two of them as she could. Bud was just wanting a companion and made friends with Fred's dog, a bulldog with a kind nature. Bud and the dog loved to play together. Mini would stay clear of the both of them. She had climbed up onto the top of a partial greenhouse Andy had put up to shelter his boat. She was growling as Andy chunked rocks at her. Leigh hollered at Andy to stop; that was cruel. Mini came down and stayed the night, but would not come to Andy. She let Leigh pet on her, but she was visibly upset with him. The next day she disappeared. He had her for over 10 years and was never to be seen again.

Leigh was having a hard time keeping her bills paid, and Andy did not help nor willingly want to despite that he stayed at her house. He had leased out the greenhouses on his side of the creek to the family that bought his father's house. He did care that he added to her costs, her bills for everything, and she needed his help. She did his laundry. She cooked and cleaned up after him at her home. He bought her wine and occasionally some groceries, which he ate. Andy decided he was going to pay her electric bill, but she would have to pay him back and give him her stainless-steel side by side refrigerator from her foreclosed house. He kept telling her on the phone to, "Go and measure the refrigerator!" She thought, "Wow, what an ass. It won't even fit in your doorway let alone your house!" Leigh's sister Debbie and Gregory ended up helping her pay her electric bill.

Andy had just finished making a vat of his beloved chili and had left it in Leigh's refrigerator. She really did not care for chili but she thought the raccoons who frequented her screened porch for leftover cat kibble would enjoy dipping their little black hands into it, making orange chili prints all over with little black noses turned orange with sauce as they pivoted into the big pot now serving every evening until gone.

Leigh decided to take in an older German Shepherd from an animal shelter. Andy had also found a companion and slept with one of his former high school classmates, Deb. He had discovered online social media and was reaching out to his old flames from high school. The thing about old high school relations, it's not like these "friends" have changed, they've just learned to hide it better.

Back in Dallas, Leigh had helped Rodney sell a house that he had in shambles. She brought him 12 offers on it and he finally accepted one, selling it. His wife, Beverly was glad to be rid of it but Rodney was not wanting to see it go and had stalled the process as long as he could. She was as good as she could be about it. Rodney was not being realistic. He finally saw what had transpired after he realized how many offers Leigh had actually brought him, having to name them off to him. He felt bad and had an old silver Ford Ranger that was the same little truck from years ago that his stepfather came and rescued her in when Rodney and Leigh broke up. The truck had been torn up by Rodney's stepchildren, and he just wanted it gone. It had caused a lot of grief between him and his wife and she was glad to be rid of it. The problem initially was the water pump, followed by the tail light, timing belt, gear shift, clutch, and now the title was still in Rodney's dead stepfather's name and all the paperwork had been destroyed by one of his stepchildren. It took Leigh a year to get the title in her name, having to call supervisors to instruct the local county tax office on the procedure. Andy never believed Leigh and thought she got the truck for sexual acts with Rodney. Rodney would have liked that, but his wife, Beverly wouldn't have. Leigh went back to Rodney's for the camper top and it even had a Horseshoe Bend sticker on it. Leigh did not know David had a house in her neighborhood. He had lived there before she did, and now it was like the little truck came home. Andy saw the value of this little truck and had tried to convince Leigh to put the title in his name so he could put insurance on it, as if she could trust him again.

In East Texas, Leigh had a dairy farm listed for almost a year and had it under contract. The seller had to fly in from the Netherlands, and Leigh was set to meet up with both the buyer and seller. Andy wanted Leigh to meet him at his little lake camper. He started to become amorous, wanting her to have sex with him before her meeting with her clients. Leigh laughed at him. "What is up with you?" He was jealous and wanting control. He was unbelievable and Leigh didn't have the time. He wanted her to come right back after her appointment. Leigh did, and he made her a nice lunch and then picked a fight with her over the appointment she had, over her important clients. What did he think she was selling? He could not see Leigh how she really was. He could not see her as anything other than something subservient and sexual and thought that's how others saw her as well, as a professional, but in the wrong profession.

During Leigh's time alone, she painted the borders of her kitchen walls with treetops and a mural on the wall by her refrigerator with an old oak tree in the woods. Leigh painted the downstairs bath with a mural depicting a scene underwater, surrounded by the fish in the lake including the 11-pound Bass she caught named Magda, some Crappie, and Perch swimming around, looking up to see the ducks paddling by from below. She painted the upstairs bath. It was a field of local flowers with all of the butterflies from Andy's greenhouses and some hummingbirds with a few lizards chatting at the base of the wainscoting.

Thanksgiving turkey time, Andy was back. He bought a larger trailer with the income from father's house and wanted to show it to Leigh. Marie and Leigh refer to it as the "pink pussy wagon". He and his friends call it the "stabbin' cabin". His friends avoided Leigh like the plague, knowing too well what had happened while she was away. She had been bombarded by Jane and Jamey pressuring her to take her grandchildren while being on the cusp of menopause. Leigh was concerned about the instability of her cycle and had taken a pregnancy test, worried about all of the alcohol consumption and any possible effects. Andy tore into her about what she was hiding. Leigh was embarrassed to talk to him, and he grabbed her pocket and made her turn it out to find a negative pregnancy test.

Andy was on the other side of that line. Leigh pulled others up as he pushed others over. He had death surrounding him with his family and friends dying. Leigh had never been around so much death without any reverence or condolences for their passing. Andy acted like it was too much trouble for him to respect the lives of those who considered him a friend. He was unbelievable to her in his selfishness and lack of decency.

It was a new year, and Leigh was trying to minimize the toxic relationships in her life starting with her daughter, Jane's access as well as Jamey. Both had created such drama, she was losing focus, fearful of having to take on her grandchildren and having to deal with Jamey' twisting of reality into his drug-addicted fog. She had been drinking too much with Andy, and there seemed to be no end. She had broken up with Andy more times then was reasonable, and on Friday the 13th, being the day before Valentine's, Andy decided that he has had enough of a girlfriend with no money. He pulled a little blue velvet bag out of his pocket and threw it at Leigh screaming that he cannot take her lies, that she never had any money, and he can't take it anymore. He storms out. The little ring he had gotten for her looked like it was a machine part, a thick washer that had been polished, still having rough edges. Be careful what you wish for and make sure you can live with it. Always remember in a rural little town, don't drink the water, and don't date the locals.

After a year and a half apart, Leigh and Andy started visiting online and put five more months together between them. Andy had sold his little storage building studio and moved into a larger camper on Lake Fork, working as a fishing guide. He sold his studio equipment and kept a safe full of collector basses and bought a yellow kit car that he had to rent a storage building as a garage for it. He had tried to find a new girlfriend. He was still making the rounds with other women, hiding his indiscretions from Leigh. One he was still tangling with would meet with him, knowing well what they both were doing. She was very artificial, had married for money and was a widow who could pick and choose when and where he could do for her. They were so much alike in their lack of morals or accountability. The artificial woman had even allowed him to store his newly acquired kit car in her garage at her convenience, but it became inconvenient and they had a tiff which resulted in Andy reaching back to Leigh.

Andy did not like being alone around the holidays. His work as a guide slowed and the winter months were cold and long. He sought companionship with Leigh once again. They spent every day together that she wasn't in Dallas. He had gained weight and was drinking beer in the afternoons and whiskey every night. He had become too fat to fit into his own clothes. He had aged considerably, showing signs of alcoholism, the coloring, texture of his skin. Andy had believed Leigh had taken an old sentimental cup of his. It was something a former love had long ago given him. He tried to find it at her house but couldn't locate it. He told her that he needed more cups for his camper, hoping she would return the lost cup, but she just gave him other ones to replace it. He took Leigh's coveted sunglasses, that he had bought unwillingly so many years before, and put them behind her car tire. She located them, crushed. He seemed to feel guilty after she found them. This time he replaced them without issue, after all, it was Christmas. So many petty things go on between two people over so many years.

Leigh was as she had always been, too trusting to a harmful man who's only concern was himself. He had been seeking, testing, and auditioning for another woman. Leigh had just pulled back, hibernating, just wanting to recover from being hurt so much, so many times. He had been playing music with a bunch Leigh intentionally avoided, still hurting from the previous group and the death of his band member, Brent. The latest band was playing at a little winery out in East Texas, and Andy decided that Leigh should accompany him knowing his little dalliance, the artificial woman who kept his car in her garage would be there. She had all of the artificial cosmetics done on a regular basis that her dead husband's money could buy. She arrived later at Andy's show. Leigh had already been slighted by one of Andy's band members, the singer, a woman who sang off-key, not able to perform at Andy's level. This artificial woman was the singer's best friend, who had set up with Andy a year before. It was a cat pissing contest. Andy had to perform while she and her little girlfriend were at one table and Leigh was at another. Andy was very nervous. Leigh was not one to tolerate another woman, and he knew it. Leigh was never approached, but the tension was very palatable. Andy's life had become more saturated in alcohol. The months that Leigh and Andy were together were a blur. He would not stay at Leigh's home, but instead, had to be at his camper. She did as she had done before, supported him in what he wanted, how he wanted, but he didn't want her drinking wine. She would cook for him, clean up and buy groceries for their meals as she always had. He wanted her drinking beer followed by shots of whiskey. It was too much for her. She would tell him no, wait until the weekend for the drinking, but he couldn't. It was a nightly ritual, and he would continually push it on her.

He lived in his camper full-time and typically was alone in the park during the week. He had made friends with several weekenders, families who came around on holidays and long weekends. As a prank, a couple of the guys along with their teenage son, got Andy's spare key and woke him early, unannounced, scaring him, unaware he kept a loaded gun. Andy had a fit. As a result, he decided to barge in on his friends in their camper. Two of the men just laughed at him, so Andy decided he would strip in front of them and chase the teenager around the camper, naked. The men laughed even louder seeing Andy's miniature penis. The more they retold the story, the smaller they claimed it was, saying that they had never seen a penis that small on a full-grown man. This explained so much of his behavior.

The woman Andy had seen in-between Andy and Leigh's last break had all of the things Andy had longed for, she was slim, attractive and had money. Leigh was no further along financially than she had been when Andy broke up with her previously, but he couldn't find the same intensity he had known with Leigh in this other woman. He couldn't replace her so easily. Andy would line up a prospective woman, but once she would see how he lived, in a camper, saturated in alcohol, she would become just another friend.

At another concert, Andy invited another old musician he had known to play New Year's Eve together. The in-between woman didn't make an appearance, and it was a great show despite being at the singer's restaurant, the other woman's close friend. Leigh did not have to compete with her that night.

Weeks later the other woman was at another show at the winery. Andy was gathering equipment. Leigh did what she could do to help being very tense about having to see the other woman again. Leigh ruined Andy's evening just as it had started. She had a seizure. One of the waiters saw her and knew she was suffering, hunched at a table against a wall. Andy thought she was just drunk, but she had not been drinking. They called an ambulance and carted her off to a local hospital emergency room. She had to stop. She couldn't carry on like Andy. It almost killed her. Her blood pressure was deadly. Andy was upset, but didn't really want to make any adjustments, knowing that Leigh was at risk and shouldn't be left alone. He didn't care unless it directly affected him. He did pay to have Leigh see his doctor, or at least his doctors' nurse practitioner to get Leigh on some blood pressure medication, but this was not what she needed. She had to stop the hard alcohol and so much drinking. He wouldn't and pushed on her more than before. He didn't care if it killed her, or if she was alone to have another seizure. He couldn't be bothered. She was amazed and awoken by this. She stayed away. She went to her daughter's to have a break from him. He filled his time with other options, other women, teasing her that he wasn't being faithful...to his diet. He spent most of his time trying to find a Thunderbird. Dozens of years ago, he had to sell one when he divorced and was still looking for a replacement. He was always looking for a replacement. He thought if he drove a flashy car, he could attract attention. He replaced his yellow kit car with an old Thunderbird painted candy apple red. He had a fancy car, but no garage to keep it in. He still could not find anyone with money that would hang out with him in his camper. At least, it wouldn't last. He worked as a guide on the lake known for his full-blown alcoholism and having a revolving door for female guests in his camper. Leigh saw him drinking hard liquor every night now. He wanted her to drink along with him, but she couldn't keep it up. It was too much for her health. It was too much and she couldn't stand the other women too. It was over. He was inviting death.

Chapter 8. Death and Disguise

Leigh saw Andy, sneaking off to tempt other women. With her health now in jeopardy, she refused to endure his promiscuous behavior. He couldn't really do much anymore sexually. It seemed as though the risky behavior aroused him. He was off of his game and could chase, but not execute. Leigh was home alone. She had tried to keep her life quiet. She had to detox from Andy. She was unable to recover from the damage. The seizure was a precursor to a stroke. The stroke occurred when Leigh was alone. Her daughter Marie couldn't reach her mother, so she made the trip out from Dallas to check on her. Leigh's dog Bear was mournfully laying at Leigh's side. Marie notified every one of her mother's passing.

In a little Catholic church, there are white flowers on the altar. Dozens of little glass votive tea lights are glowing in the dim early morning light. There are two candelabras with candlesticks burning, flanking a little, simple, wooden coffin centered at the base of the sanctuary. The doors of the church are being propped open. Just inside the nave is a small cloth covered table. There is a clear glass vase and 5 white long stem roses upon it. It is almost sunrise as the guests start to arrive. Marie is at the entrance, greeting everyone, handing them a little, folded brochure with a prayer and a picture of Leigh with one of her German Shepherds inside.

Everyone is making their way inside, scattered about in the empty echo of the church. It was surprising to see who had been able to attend. All of Leigh's exes were present. All of her ex-boyfriends began to mingle with her family. All of Leigh's sisters were able to come. Jeanie, dressed in a tight short, low cut black dress and stilettos made a line for Huston, recognizing him after all of the years, giving him a tight squeeze. He blinkingly blushes. He looks the same, but a little greyer, just as heavy in a black suit. Gregory, older and more gaunt, uncomfortable, tugging at his neck in a suit and tie, quietly introduces himself to Julie as tears well up in his eyes. Julie dressed in a conservative black dress asks him if he was the married one. He nods in agreement. Andy, dressed in a white shirt and dark slacks, scoots next to Jeanie and Huston, giving Jeanie a hug, she squints, in a hushed voice, "We met out at her lake house," he nods. Jeanie looks past him and spots Fred all alone. He has become very heavy and his hair is still long but silver and receding, uncomfortable in his dark clothes. She waves over to him, excited to see him as he is to see her "Oh my God, Fred!" Angie and her husband are cheerful smiling, making their way into a row in the back. Jamie and her daughters file in, sitting in a front pew. Debbie and her new husband are meeting Kenny just inside the vestibule. Kenny, dressed in a dark grey suit has gray, short hair and a huge gut with shirt buttons bulging. He has become his father. He recalls how many years ago it was since they had met up with Leigh, recalling his 78' Thunderbird and her old 280z and how many they could fit into that little 2 seaters. They quietly laugh. Rodney enters with his wife, Beverly, both in black. He reaches over to hug Debbie. Jane is outside in front, crying loudly as her boys stand hopelessly at their mother's side. She is waiting for her daughter, Ashley's arrival. Her sobs were audible from inside.

Angie and Daniel, their son and daughter fill the pew on the back row. Marie, Rick, Ryan, and Liz are seated in a back-pew opposite. Marie walks down the center aisle up to the podium at the base of the sanctuary.

She addresses the crowd "We all knew Leigh in our own way, if anyone would like to step forward and share a story, please do."

The first one to the podium is Gregory. "Hi, I'm Gregory. I don't know a lot of you. I wasn't in Leigh's life very long, but I have heard so much about many of you, especially her daughters and her sisters. This is a woman that I loved and that loved me. Had things been different, we would have spent the rest of our lives together. To her sisters, you are lucky to have called her sister. To her former boyfriends, you don't know what you have lost. Leigh was a terrific girl. She brightened up everybody and everything. We had so many great times together in Hawaii. She was the love of my life, and I cannot believe she is no longer with us," he steps back, in tears, too upset to continue. Andy had never met Gregory and goes up to the podium, glaring at him competitively. Bending the mic for optimum effect "Hi, I'm Andy. I knew Leigh from East Texas. She was a handful. She could fish better than most men. We would pull up to a spot that another boat had just pulled off of and she would get a tug as the other boats just watched, one after another. She could fish." He takes a gulp, chin out and steps down. Huston rolls his eyes in disgust. Fred steps up. "I knew Leigh when she was a little-red-headed teenager working at California Steak House out in Georgia, he braggingly boasts "I was her first love. We would cook together and cruise in my old truck

eons ago." Fred steps back giving way as Kenny follows. "I'm Kenny. Leigh and me would hang out in Oak Cliff back in the days when the Cowboys won the Super Bowl. She was great. We went all over the place in her little, black 280z, flying down the highway! She loved that car! She had not kept in touch, and I had no idea that she had been sick. It's just unbelievable," he stated, shaking his head, dropping back. Jamey steps up "I'm Jamey. Leigh and me have two beautiful daughters together and five grandchildren. She was a great mom. She will be missed." He wipes his eye. Rodney steps up "Leigh was a loving mother to her daughters, she was smart, fun, and put her girls first. She was always fun to be around and I will miss her, the one that got away. Rodney's wife, sitting in a pew, squirms upon hearing this from her husband as he bites his lower lip, heading back to her. Huston finally steps up after assessing the crowd, the other men in particular. "I'm Huston. As the rest of you all know Leigh, I believe I knew her the best. She was a fiery little thing who always did what she wanted. She had the body of a fourteenyear-old. She would never take my advice and would do just the opposite just for spite. Ya couldn't help but love her with her long red hair. She was fearless and would take on things others twice her size would avoid. She took me on for a time and what a time we had. She was truly the best love I have known, and the sex was great!" Gregory heckles him "Ya think so, well I know about you, you're that disbarred attorney who couldn't hold his temper!" Huston throws his head up, raising a brow "Really, you're that married damned Yankee! What the hell do you care!" Gregory retorts "They called you Hucifer and they were right" Marie steps up to mediate the situation, hands out as she glares at the two with a scoff.

Jane wiping her eyes steps up to the podium. She summarizes each as the order each knew Leigh "I recognize who everyone is: Fred the virgin slayer, Kenny the dropout, Jamey my druggy, absentee daddy, Rodney the fun drunk, Huston the disbarred felon, the married Yankee Gregory, and Andy, the singing cowboy. What a bunch you all are. And did any of you even know who or what she wanted or even care? She didn't want to marry any of you. She had sex with all of you. She wasn't after your money or fame. She just wanted to be loved. She didn't ever expect anything out of any of you. She made everyone laugh. She made everyone crazy. She was my Mom. Jane looks out at a sparse collection scattered throughout the church pews. She shakes her head and steps down.

Marie replaces Jane at the podium "My mom was everything, Mom just wanted to be loved, not to be lonely, to have someone she could depend on that could depend on her." Marie continues, "Would each of her sisters take a rose from the vase Marie states, pointing to the little table down the aisle opposite, and please place it on top of her coffin." Marie opens the coffin. Inside, Leigh is dressed in gothic black attire with her long red hair. Marie looks back to the crowd, biting her lip. The sisters gather at the small table, each taking a white rose. Julie proceeds first, followed by Angie, Jamie, and Debbie. Jeanie was busy visiting in the pew and makes her

144

way lastly, hastily cutting in front of Debbie. Each forms a procession of siblings and follow behind Julie's lead. Julie places her rose on the top of the coffin, as she dabs a tissue to her eyes. Angie has a half gleeful look, nonchalantly placing her rose on top of the first. Jamie looks saddened as she does the same. Jeanie is a little behind, adjusting her hair and tugging at her cleavage. She proceeds as all eyes are upon her, standing straight, she sticks her chest out and sashays down the aisle in her stilettos. She reaches to place her rose inside the coffin, on top of Leigh. Leigh winks at her. Jeanie screams, pulling back shouting, "That Bitch! Oh my God, that Bitch! Leigh, you Bitch!", the other sisters quickly rally around Jeanie as they try to drag her out of the church, down the center aisle. She is screaming like a crazy woman. Debbie tosses her rose on the top of the pile and tries to join the others to contain Jeanie. Marie quickly shuts the lid of the coffin. Marie hears a muffled sneeze from inside the coffin, looking up to see if anyone else noticed, but everyone is distracted by Jeanie as her tirade echoes from the entrance of the church. The crowd is exiting, dumbfounded by Jeanie's display. Organ music begins playing Ava Maria until the church is now empty again.

A hearse pulls up in front of the church. Ed is behind the wheel smoking a cigar with the window cracked. Puffs of smoke waft out into the morning air. Jeanie's loud hissy has spilled onto the veranda as her sisters scramble in heels and black dresses to take her away. Ed watches from a safe distance, humored by it all.

Marie is in the church alone at the coffin. She looks around, making sure that she is alone and knocks three times on the lid.

It's a sunny, beautiful day on the North Shore of Kauai, in Hanalei. Ed is lounging in a folding chair with toes in the sand, puffing on a cigar with a folded book in his hand, looking up to the blue-green ocean with a chuckle of contentment. Ed sees a very dark tanned muscular twentysomething-year-old man wearing little swim trunks and a smile carrying a long surfboard into the water, wading in gentle waist-high waves. He is with a pale, white, little, redheaded woman, teaching her how to stand on a surfboard.